WHISPERS, WHISKERS, & WEDDING NIGHT

WHISPERS, WHISKERS, & WEDDING NIGHT

Cozy Clowder Chronicles Book 1.1

Imogen Knowed

Imogen Knowed

ISBN: 979-8-9874825-3-7

Dedication

This story is dedicated to all those who couldn't get enough of this anxious little throuple.

And, of course, Megan Thee Stallion.

Content Warnings

This book has explicit descriptions of sexual acts.

There is a casual mention of the following, with none described in detail:
- Childhood assault and abuse
- Suicide
- Stalking
- Attempted murder

Events in this book center around various mental health crises and coming to terms with sexuality.

Body shaming, ageism, and some ableist language are also present.

If you have any questions or comments about these content warnings, feel free to contact me. You can find me at:
https://www.instagram.com/imogenknowed/

Before You Proceed

This short story is set in the Cozy Clowder Chronicles universe and does not stand alone. It should be read after Whispers, Whiskers, & Wine (Cozy Clowder Chronicles Book 1).

Spoiler-y Refresher of Whispers, Whiskers, & Wine:

Adley found two "cats" in her backyard. However, they were not "cats" but Ailura shifters—people who can shift between ailo (cat-like) and anthro (humanoid) forms. They found their way to her backyard through portals from a different universe. They purred for her, signaling she was their fated mate.

Despite their various mental health challenges, the three eventually formed a deep bond, solidifying their relationship as a "clowder" and having a wedding/mate-marking ceremony in the Epilogue. The events within this story occur directly after the Epilogue as they begin their honeymoon.

1

MARSHALL

"I know, I know, my thirsty Ezronies. You'll all miss me terribly, but I'm a married man now. I have to take care of my mates…if you know what I mean," Ezra says to the phone above his head. He walks around the room, his enthusiasm abundant even after our long day.

His energy is making my anxiety about our trip worse. I frown as I look at all the bags splayed across the bed. Until about an hour ago, I had these bags perfectly organized and packed.

"And this, my gorgeous followers, is what happens when you marry not one, but two organization nerds—packing cubes and spreadsheets," Ezra says, allowing the camera to peek at the bags behind him. I quickly close the suitcase containing sex toys, so it doesn't appear on the feed.

"Speaking of, say 'hi' to your adoring fans, Marsh!" he says, jumping on me and wrapping his arm around my shoulder.

I roll my eyes and sigh, "I don't have fans."

"You're right. Sorry, Marsh. I should have said fan. BrandyX32 says 'hi,'" he laughs. I glance at the screen, and it fills with hearts. Suddenly, I appear as if I am wearing a digital pompadour and shiny glasses. I wave my hand in front of my face to make it disappear, only for cowboy hats to pop on our heads. A rocket flies in front of us. It's a chaotic mess of interactions. I avert my gaze. I hate when he goes live on TikTok. I can't watch these streams. There's too much going on, and it stresses me out. I swat away the little animated dog licking my face. Fucking dogs.

Knowing I can only take so much of being included in his stream, Ezra smacks my ass with his free hand. He rotates so that the camera no longer captures me or the bags, and I relax slightly.

I lean over to recount my socks, but he grabs my tail from root to tip. I startle and almost hiss at him, but he winks at me, melting my resolve. He's being significantly more sexually aggressive with me today than usual. I'm getting a sense of what it must be like to be Adley. I'm unsure if this change is due to our mate-bonding or mating season. Either he's more comfortable in the relationship elevation, or he's just fucking horny. I rub at my crotch

1

and suspect, based on my body's reaction, it's a combination.

Traveling makes me anxious. Packing makes me anxious. Ezra flitting about is making me anxious. All of this makes me anxious. Adley told me when I feel like this I should "focus on the now" (whatever the fuck that means), look at my surroundings, and count my breaths.

Ok. Just try it, Marshall. The morning light spills through the bedroom curtains like a thin golden ribbon. It lands perfectly on the suitcase holding my clothing. I stare at the light beam and steady my breath. I consider curling up in my suitcase, hiding, and letting my mates handle the rest of the trip preparations.

If I'm being honest, I'm not just anxious about the trip; I'm also worried about what the trip entails. Ezra has been dropping hints all day about his honeymoon plans with me. Not the king of subtlety, he's said things like, "I've got plans for that ass," and I don't have to be great with idioms to get what he's implying.

I know the body struggles to tell the difference between excitement and anxiety. Both cause similar physiological responses. I'm trying to convince myself that my heart's racing is exaggerated by excited anticipation, not just fear.

"No, I can't tell you all where we are going! I can't have you showing up on the doorstep while I'm off on my honeymoon! I'll only be away for two weeks. You'll all be fine. And don't worry. Stephanie has a bunch of things planned in my absence. She's got some blooper reels and greatest hits all scheduled out to keep you thirsty dolls quenched while I'm gone," he says to the stream.

Adley leans into the room, her long hair up in a messy bun on top of her head, emphasizing the gentle curve of her neck. I wish I had my head resting in that curve while I read my book, rather than standing here recounting these socks. She taps her wrist, indicating it's time for him to stop streaming, and disappears—presumably back to the bathroom, to continue her packing. Well, unpacking and repacking, I should say.

We packed last night. But I'm not the only one who gets anxiety before traveling. My anxiety manifests as a racing heart, over-preparation, and a tendency to retreat into my own head. Adley's anxiety manifests as neurotic unpacking, repacking, and quadruple checking, with an energy that could rival Ezra's.

Ezra instinctively glances at his watch, but I don't know why. He never uses it to tell the time. He just wears it because it makes him feel "bougie," as Adley calls it. He tells time via a series of alarms set on his phone and Adley or me telling him what time it is.

"Welp, the goddess of time and calendars is telling me it's time to head out! I'll see you in two weeks! Maybe I'll have a tan? Who knows," he says with a shrug. He blows a kiss and signs off.

Ezra flops on the bed, his persona drops, and his energy completely drains from him. The suitcases and packing cubes splayed all over the bed bounce in response to his weight, causing further disorganization. Sigh.

"Fuck, bro, I need this vacation. I am so tired," Ezra yawns.

His presence, now calmed, comforts me. I push a suitcase aside and sit gently next to him on the bed, trying not to make more of a mess. I run my fingers through his hair, petting him in those long strokes he enjoys. "Yeah, you've been working hard. It's good you have Stephanie now."

Stephanie has replaced me as Ezra's personal assistant. She does all his administrative work and can do a lot more than I could. She's kind of amazing.

"Sorry about the last-minute stream. You know how Steph gets," Ezra says. He turns into my touch, purring and hugging his tail to his chest.

During our wedding reception, Stephanie ran up to Ezra, showing him articles and forum posts of people speculating that Ezra wasn't getting married but going to rehab. He initially said he didn't care. However, once she mentioned his brand and approval rating, he quickly turned from blasé to high-strung.

Unfortunately, that meant instead of leaving for our honeymoon directly after our reception, Ezra had to do "damage control, bro." He posted a picture during the wedding reception and, after changing clothes, immediately jumped on a live stream. He's spent the last hour telling his followers about the reception and assuring them they'd have content in his absence.

At first, Adley and I cuddled on the couch and read while we waited for him to finish his work. But before I could finish my first page, she rose from her seat, rushed to a bag waiting by the door, and pulled out items to ensure they were in the bag. "Did you pack your X, Marshall? How about Y? Did I pack Z?" she asked about every single object that crossed her mind, panicking that we forgot something—everything. I tried reassuring her that we triple-checked last night and reminded her of the system we devised to avoid this exact scenario. However, my reassurance did nothing but frustrate her. She had to check with her own eyes. So, I acquiesced instead of fighting with my mate on my honeymoon. And now I'm humoring her obsessive behavior by assisting with the unpacking and repacking endeavor. Thus, Adley's two suitcases, my one, and Ezra's five have all their contents arranged around our bedroom. I'm trying to keep our stuff as organized as possible in the aftermath of my mates' emotional storms.

Instead of complaining to Ezra about how all of this has actually caused me a significant amount of discomfort, and that I, too, have apprehensions and worries, I say, "It's okay. We'll still get there at a good time."

He stretches and turns to me, his gaze softening as he places his hand on my thigh. "Tonight's gonna be epic," he says with a smirk. I know what he's thinking.

"Thank God you're already dressed, otherwise we'd never make it there," I joke, trying to deflect my mood with humor the way he always does.

"Even a bad hair day wouldn't make me miss tonight, Marshmallow."

I continue to stroke his hair and run my fingers up the tip of his ear. Comforting him brings me comfort, and I already feel a lot better.

"Watch it, bro. You keep that up, and we will be late," he grins.

I laugh and look at the items spread around the bed. Ezra follows my gaze and says, "You're still packing? I thought you had a whole system." He gestures to the open laptop, which displays the spreadsheet representing our packing list.

"Adley's in anxiety mode and undid it all," I say.

"Oh, shit. I'm sorry you had to deal with that by yourself." He sits up and further assesses the controlled chaos. "Honestly, I kind of love that it's going to be Adley that makes us late for once," Ezra chuckles.

Adley rushes into the room. She runs her finger down the screen displaying the spreadsheet, tracing and checking our list for the one-millionth time.

Her energy breaks into the calm that was forming between Ezra and me. If it didn't stress me out, I'd laugh at how she and Ezra have switched energy roles for the day. Something about travel and packing puts her on edge, no matter how much we prepare. I've only seen her like this once before—the last time we went on a trip together. I hoped my spreadsheet and over-preparedness would have saved her some of this anxiety, but alas, my planning can never seem to get ahead of Adley's mood shifts.

"Marshall, I really feel like we forgot something," she says, for maybe the one-hundredth time today, nervously tapping her finger against her bottom lip and staring blankly at the piles behind me. Ezra will calm her for me. He's good at that.

EZRA

"Babe, the two of you spent a week putting that spreadsheet together. You haven't forgotten anything. Besides, if you did happen to forget something, we're going to have the car. We're not going to the middle of nowhere. You can just buy whatever you forgot," I say, standing and wrapping my arms around her waist. I press my dick against that perfect ass she was poking in my face when she bent to look at the laptop.

"I know, I know," she says, visibly calming as I nuzzle into her. Nothing like a stiff dick against an anxious ass to calm it. "But I'm just worried we'll forget something irreplaceable."

Adley and Marshall devised a color-coded packing system, with each of us having a designated cube color. Mine, the green, outnumbers the pink and black ones by a long shot. We have everything we need. More than we need. I won't say that most of the "more" is sitting in green bags, because I don't really need to. We all know it to be true.

"Babe, the only irreplaceable things coming on this trip are you and him," I say, thumbing at Marshall. I expect he's perked up at the callout, but don't turn to check. "And me, obviously," I say with an eyebrow waggle. I calm my voice and say, "Remember, you get anxious about travelling. This is just a feeling, not a fact, yeah?"

Throwing these phrases from her therapy sessions at her generally does the trick, but first, she's gotta fight me just a little more on it. She's probably going to bring up the toothbrush incident. "Someone has to make sure we don't end up buying toothbrushes at a gas station like last time." Yep, there it is.

"I packed my toothbrush," I protest, setting my phone down to zip the last of my designer luggage—a chaotic jumble of expensive clothes crammed together without apparent order, but folded meticulously to ensure a wrinkle-free travel experience. "Probably."

I slip my hand down the front of her pants, and she bumps me away, laughing, "Ezra, come on."

"Hey, don't blame me, babe. Marsh was rubbing my ear making eyes at me then you came in and threw that ass in my face. We can get to the cabin whenever; who cares if we're late? Let's start the honeymoon sex right now," I smirk, trying to pull her to the bed with me. If I can get her to sit on my face, that should ease some of this tension in her. Her eyes, gray as the winter lake we're preparing to visit, soften as they land on me, and I think, perhaps, my attempts may succeed.

She turns and looks at Marshall to see his reaction to my propositions, but I don't know why. That dude is always down to fuck when I am.

"I am interested to see if your pussy tastes like Ezra's cum now that he's mate marked you," Marshall says with that scientific dorkiness he can't seem to escape.

"Bro, how can you always manage to make the sexiest thing sound so profoundly unsexy?"

"Oh? How should I have said it instead?"

I reflect for a moment, and…my brain is too frazzled by the idea that her pussy may taste like his cum to think of something. "I don't know, bro, I'll get back to you when the blood has returned to my brain," I say, standing again to press my erection back into Adley.

"It's already going to be dark by the time we arrive. I really don't want to be any later than we already are," she says with a whimper as I reach back into her pants to flick her clit again. While my attempts to get laid didn't work, it seems my attempts to convince her to stop worrying about packing have. I throw a satisfied grin at Marshall, and he gives me a tight appreciative one in return, silently thanking me for the assist with Adley's anxiety.

"Alright, babe. We'll keep it in our pants for now," I say and kiss her on the top of her head. "I'll start putting some bags in the car. Which ones are ready?"

2

ADLEY

As I enter the garage, I cross-reference the spreadsheet Marshall and I compiled from my phone with the one running continuously through my head. I'm terrified we forgot something, but Marshall and Ezra convinced me to let it go. The fact that the sun will probably be set by the time we get to Duluth gnaws at me more than the idea that we forgot something. Ezra's right. I can just buy whatever we forgot.

Marshall looms behind me, carrying the last of the bags, awaiting my word and likely suspecting I'll make him open the bags again.

Ezra peeks at us from behind the car, rubbing the back of his head. That grin he wears when he knows he's fucked something up is plastered all over his face.

"Ok, so, ummm...Marsh, I need your help," he says as Marshall approaches him from the side of the car.

"Ezra," Marshall says with a defeated sigh when he reaches the back of the car. The hatchback is open, and suitcases are spilling out of not only the car, but the garage.

Ezra chuckles, "So we've all learned something today. Packing a car is not my strong suit. Let's consider that, in itself, a win."

"Jeez, Ez, you really are bad at this," I say, impressed at how he managed to precariously position the few suitcases he did actually get into the car.

Marshall sighs and undoes all of Ezra's "work" by removing the luggage and placing them, along with the others that had spilled out, in a neat stack on the garage floor.

Ezra's ears lie flat on his head, obviously feeling chastised by Marshall's loaded sigh. When Marshall places the last suitcase on the floor, he notices Ezra's demeanor. Marshall smacks him on the ass, saying, "You're lucky you're cute."

Ezra perks up at the compliment, but a yawn overtakes him before he can say something quippy. We help Marshall pack the car by handing him bags as he points them out to us. He's worked out a precise packing system that only he is privy to. Whenever Marshall points at a bag bigger than a breadbox, Ezra nudges me out of the way if I try to reach for it, insisting that I not "strain yourself, babe."

Another yawn escapes Ezra, as he butt bumps me away from a heavy case and carries it to Marshall's impatient, outstretched hands. I pull him into an embrace, running my hands down the length of his spine and relishing the feel of his hard body against mine. I caress his chin and coo, "Why don't you take a nap on the drive up?"

Dismissing my suggestion, he yawns, "I'm good, babe, I wanna listen to that book with you on the drive. I need to know who the murderer is."

"Come on, Ez. You look like you're about to pass out." Before he gets offended at the comment, I add, "I'm not saying you look tired; you look fabulous." Then I clarify, while placing the bag I'm holding into Marshall's waiting hands, by saying, "You just keep yawning."

Ezra opens his mouth to protest, but Marshall, while placing a suitcase in the back, says, "We can't have you falling asleep mid-coitus, old man." The way Marshall looks behind himself, with his ass high in the air is super hot. If I didn't know any better, I'd think he was trying to seduce Ezra. He's officially seduced me.

"Fine," Ezra says, rolling his eyes. He approaches Marshall, still bent over the back, pushing a suitcase into the car. Ezra bends over Marshall and presses against his ass. He runs Marshall's tail in his hand and whispers into his ear, "Don't worry, bro, I'll make sure I have all the energy I need for you tonight."

Slightly taken aback by this overt sexual advance, I chuckle, "I thought the mate marking ceremony was supposed to make you two less horned up. Not more horned up."

"Oh, I did say that, didn't I?" Ezra asks, now jamming his pelvis into me and grinding on my hip.

"Yes, you did. When you explained all this claiming and mate marking stuff to me."

Ezra just laughs and says, "Unfortunately, you married us in the middle of mating season. It's like our dicks are attuned to February, regardless of the universe."

A bark startles Ezra, causing him to jump away from me and hiss. Marshall leaps from his bent position to turn toward the source of the noise, growling. Ezra and Marshall's eyes lock on our neighbor James and his dog, Max, strolling across the opening of our driveway. Ezra and Marshall stand at full attention, their tails raised high and fluffed out. They look about as on edge as they did when we ran into my ex, Bryce, in Target.

"Sorry about that! You three heading out on your honeymoon?" James asks, not stopping his walk—he learned long ago that stopping with Max in front of our house is a decidedly bad idea.

"Yeah, we are," I say, with a wave and a smile.

"Well, have fun! I'll keep an eye on the house for ya. Let ya know if Max spots any more stalkers lurking about," he says with a distinctly Minnesotan accent.

"Thanks so much!" I say, glancing at the guys, still stiff as boards.

"Bye," James and I say as he continues his walk. He pulls Max with all his strength, as the dog tries to tug toward our garage. Max seems to have a real affinity for Ezra, despite Ezra calling him "Max-imum Suckage" and refusing to let the dog within 5 feet of him. However, Ezra has conceded to "allowing" the dog to cross our driveway after the dog stopped a pair of fans from taking pictures through our window a few months ago.

Once James turns the corner, the guys finally relax and return to packing the garage, as if nothing even happened. Ezra hefts one of his bags, which weighs considerably more than any of mine or Marshall's. He drags it toward Marshall, whose ass is hanging out the back of the car again.

"Marsh, if you ever start that OnlyFans account, you could post pics bending over and packing car trunks. Focus in on that demo group that's into tight asses and organization. You could really corner that niche market," Ezra says, as Marshall's tail whips back and forth, hitting Ezra's leg. Ezra pulls out his phone and leans sideways, making sure Marshall's ass is in the shot. Presumably, once the light hits his wavy locks just right, he lifts his hand, revealing the wedding band that symbolizes his bond with Marshall, and snaps a selfie.

Marshall, too lost in his quest to perfectly pack our car, doesn't acknowledge the comment. He is transforming the back of our modest SUV into a masterpiece of spatial efficiency—"luggage Tetris," Ezra calls it. He positions each bag to maximize the space, with the heaviest items at the bottom and tonight's necessities at the top.

With the last bag in place, Marshall steps back, proudly assessing his work. He closes the trunk with a satisfying thunk and turns to Ezra. "I made room for your seventeen unnecessary pairs of shoes," he tells Ezra in a tone only Ezra and I can tell is playful jabbing—others tend to read it as outright annoyance.

"They're all necessary!" Ezra counters. "And there are only twelve pairs."

I push Ezra toward the back car door, saying, "Alright, you can go lie down now. Marshall already put your bed in the back seat." Ezra lets me push him, but leans back to say to Marshall, "Aww, thanks, bro." He opens the door to reveal the cat bed designed to let him safely travel.

"Ezra, before you fall asleep, I need you to text me the location. We can't get there if you keep it a secret forever," Marshall says. Ezra planned the entire trip and, while he told us everything about what we'd be doing and where we'd be going, he wanted to surprise us with one piece: where we'd be staying.

"I wanna see!" I say, peaking over Ezra's shoulder as he texts Marshall.

Ezra hands me his phone. "The listing describes it as a luxurious woodland retreat with panoramic lake views," he says, watching my face for my reaction.

"Oh, wow! It's beautiful," I exclaim, leaning into him. "I'm sorry we won't be able to see the sunset from those windows now." If I hadn't made us late with my need to double-check the luggage, we could have watched the sunset tonight.

Ezra kisses my neck, reassuring me, and says, "Nonsense, babe. We'll be there for almost two weeks. We'll see plenty of sunsets from those windows."

He looks around for a minute, trying to decide where to transform, but I decide for him. "Go ahead, I'll get your clothes," I say, hugging him and standing on my tiptoes to kiss his cheek.

"Thanks, babe," he says, leaning to receive my kiss, then returning it with his own. He transforms and leaps into the car, leaving his clothes in a pile on the garage floor. I grab them and he meows at me.

"What'd he say?" I ask Marshall. His shadow moves methodically at the back of the car, having reopened the trunk to reposition the luggage. There must have been a flaw in his perfectly placed luggage design.

"He said you can't just bundle them up like that, they'll wrinkle," Marshall says.

I sigh, "Alright." I fold the clothes and place them in a neat pile in the other seat, ensuring he can reach them if he wants to return to his anthro form during the drive. I nestle his phone in his cup holder, meriting an appreciative head butt to my hand. I strap his specially designed harness on him (one that he can unlatch himself when he's ready to transform) and buckle him into his bed. Before I close the door, I kiss him on the head and say, "Rest. We're going to wear that fluffy old ass out otherwise."

EZRA

I pick at the fabric of my bed with my claws, making it extra comfortable before I lie down. I'm so fucking tired.

Adley was up late last night, moving our various toiletry bags back and forth between the bedroom and the bathroom. She couldn't decide where she should place them so that she wouldn't forget them for the trip, while also keeping them accessible. Her nervousness about the wedding had her focusing on the weirdest things, as she struggled to determine the "most efficient" way to do stuff. I calmed her by telling her how beautiful she was and how excited I was to finally see her in her dress. When that didn't fully work, I licked her pussy while Marshall railed into her—that knocked her out.

An hour or so later, Marshall woke in a cold sweat, nervous about standing in front of everyone during the wedding ceremony. When I finally got him to sleep, I couldn't sleep—stressing over the logistics of the whole day and checking the weather a million times.

Turns out, we're an anxious bunch.

I'm pretty happy with how the wedding and reception came together. Everything happened just as I planned—except for Stephanie coming in and claiming everyone thought I was going to rehab.

Adley looked so beautiful in her wedding dress. She wouldn't let us see it until the ceremony due to some weird human ritual focused on virginity that I don't quite understand. I certainly don't understand how it relates to my mate who got double-dicked less than 24 hours previously—definitely not a virgin—but, whatever, I won't argue with custom. I know we always say she looks like an angel, but today was extra true. The silk fabric clung to every curve, causing my fucking heart to stop. It took every muscle in my thighs to keep my dick from pointing straight at her as she walked toward Marshall and me. And, I won't tell her this, but despite all the heaters I positioned around the yard, her nipples were hard as a rock. Perfect. Flawless.

Marshall didn't say much all morning, but once he saw Adley, he started blubbering like a baby. The moment the ring was on his finger, it was like he was a changed man. He embodied both Silly Marshall and Alpha Marshall during our reception, but now he's back to his usual uptightness. Actually, now that I think about it, he's been extra quiet and jittery. I'm not quite sure why, though. Probably feeding off of Adley's energy. Or maybe I've been hitting on him a bit too aggressively. I thought he'd like it, but maybe I should cool it.

"Did you pack the extra first aid kit and various supplies just in case we get stuck in the snow?" Adley asks Marshall, running her finger down the list on her phone as she enters the driver's seat. Fuck, she's still stressing.

Marshall nods. "Yep. In the glove compartment. Restocked last night." Sigh. I love him, but this fucking guy fuels her anxiety. He approaches it with logic. But the answer is always dick and jokes—dick jokes if you're short on time. I'll let them work through it without me, though. She'll be ok once we get on the road. She struggles with transitioning between activities, but she calms down once she's in the thick of it.

"Snacks for the drive?" Adley asks, still not turning on the car, as she ensures everything is in place.

I perk up and state, "That was my job, and I have delivered magnificently." I paw toward a small cooler and a bag bulging with snacks. "Only the best for my mates," I beam.

"Ezra packed it," Marshall translates for Adley.

"That's not what I said! Translate correctly!" I snap. He doesn't.

Adley turns to look in the bag warily. "Did you include—"

"Yes, babe, I got all your gross veggie snacks," I interrupt.

She looks to Marshall, waiting for the translation. "He said he got your gross veggie snacks," he says flatly.

"Oh, so now you translate correctly?" I chuff.

"Thanks, Ez. I guess...I guess we can head out then," she says, the anxiety of the trip still latching on to her. Once we get driving, she'll feel better. She doesn't need me right now.

Marshall plugs Adley's phone into the dash, and Sexy Samuel tells her we'll be driving for two hours. We're headed up to Duluth for the majority of our honeymoon. Not my first choice, but we can't fly, so I made do. You know what sucks when you can't fly? Trying to plan a fucking honeymoon. I wanted to take my mates somewhere epic, but I suppose the largest lake in the world is epic-adjacent. Apparently, you need proper identification to get on a plane, and since I'm not private-jet rich yet, we had to pick somewhere we could drive to. I didn't want to spend the whole fucking time driving, since I'd rather spend the whole fucking time fucking, so Duluth it was.

I think I have a pretty great trip planned out. I'm excited to see the aquarium. I can't wait to see Marshall's face when he sees the otters. Dude loves cute things, and you don't get much cuter than otters, except for maybe the three of us. There's also a train museum that these two dorky mates of mine will really geek out over. I'll probably use the time there to sneak a peek at my phone, which I've promised to look at minimally.

Mostly, I'm just excited for all the lovemaking we're sure to do. What can I say? I'm a simple man with simple needs.

That's actually not true. I prefer to take my mates while eating caviar on high-thread-count sheets.

I look at my two gorgeous, now official, mates and can't believe how absolutely lucky I am to have them both. It's funny to think I wouldn't be here right now had I not been a total dickhead to Sarah—and had she not been crazy enough to push me off a balcony through the portal that brought me right to them.

Marshall pulls out his iPad, settles into his habitual posture, slumped over the tablet, prepared for the long drive. But Adley is white knuckling the steering wheel, leaning so far forward that I could slip my whole body between her and the seat. She's still on edge. I don't think Marshall notices, or if he does, he's just trying to wait out the storm, hoping to get through it unscathed. He's borne the brunt of it all afternoon, after all. Maybe I shouldn't sleep. I should help him with her.

My eyes drift closed. Fuck, I can't stay awake.

"Marsh! Put on Adley's bad bitch energy playlist. That should help her relax," I say. He simply nods and does as he's told.

I am lulled to sleep by the sounds of Megan Thee Stallion and my mate singing about being bad bitches despite their anxiety. Thanks for the assist, Megan.

3

ADLEY

"Whatcha sketching?" I ask, trying to sneak a glance at what Marshall is drawing on his iPad.

"You. The landscape. I've seen so many beautiful things today," he says wistfully. "You were so beautiful today, Adley. You always are, but I understand why your culture is enamored with weddings."

"Thanks, Marsh," I say, reaching over to stroke his vestigial ear. He leans into the touch and purrs lightly.

He's recently come to the conclusion that he's probably autistic, too, but he doesn't want to go through the process of getting officially diagnosed. "What can they tell me about myself that we don't already know?" he asked. Apparently, Ailura men are just as reluctant to seek medical attention, mental and physical, as human men. Plus, we can't even find a doctor who will see him without identification.

Marshall was reluctant to label himself as such for a while, internally insisting, "I can make eye contact!" Eventually, he asked me about it, and I explained, I can do it, but it's really uncomfortable. When he asked, "Isn't it uncomfortable for everyone?" and Ezra responded, "Nope," he had a bit of an epiphany—recognizing he was reading the "can't make eye contact" symptom literally and that, in itself, was yet another piece of evidence.

So, I've been teaching him various self-soothing strategies that work for me, and he's found that absentmindedly sketching eases his various anxieties. The feel of scratching on the paper-like surface with his pencil is the perfect stim for him.

Marshall's focus returns to the scenery, his hands still sketching despite not looking at the screen. He seems more distracted than usual, and I wonder if something is wrong. Maybe I should ask him some more questions to try to get him to open up.

"How are your videos doing?" I ask.

"The animation about gravity has only about 10k views. I think I need to rework the material. The videos might still be too advanced for children."

"Marshall, 10k views is a lot!" I say, trying to convince him.

"Not really…Ezra's—"

"Don't compare your videos to Ezra," I say. "That is a lot of views. You should be proud." He just shrugs.

Marshall is the lead animator at our studio and also does some programming, but he's been restless now that our work is only between the hours of 9 and 5. He doesn't do well with unstructured free time, and he misses his work in Physics. I wish there was a way for him to guest lecture at a nearby college, but he can't exactly get the transcripts for his Ph.D. to prove his credentials. One weekend, he locked himself in our office for two days and attempted to fully rewrite his dissertation from memory. The whole ordeal ended with him depressed and powerwashing the house before Ezra and I forced him into bed.

Perhaps fueled by his growing feelings of purposelessness, he's had baby fever for the last year. Ezra got the bright idea that maybe making educational science animations would scratch his science itch and (he didn't tell Marshall this part of the plan) keep his mind occupied enough that he'd stop obsessing over making babies. So far, it's seemed to have backfired. He decided to make educational videos for children, and now all he thinks about are kids. So, Operation Get Marshall's Mind Off Having Kids and On Science was only half successful.

Marshall glances to the back seat to see if Ezra is sleeping. He whispers, so as not to wake Ezra, "Do you think we could have the kid talk again tonight?"

I should have known asking him about his videos would spur this question. Glancing back to see if Ezra is awake, I respond, "He did say he wanted to wait until after the ceremony to discuss it again. Now's technically after the ceremony."

"Maybe it's the mating season, but it's all I can think about," Marshall says. "I want...I want to try. How do you feel now?"

Now that our game is out of early access, I don't really have any reason to protest anymore. I do want kids. I didn't want them to derail my life, though. I know some people will think I'm selfish for saying so, but I wanted to achieve my goals first. I don't have anything holding me back anymore. And, honestly, I find myself picturing tiny Marshalls and Ezras running around the house every morning when I take my pill.

"I want to, too, Marsh," I say, smiling at him.

He smiles and responds, "That makes me really happy, Adley." He pauses, reflecting, before continuing, "Now we just need to talk to Ezra.

How should we bring it up?"

"We should probably wait until after we do whatever raunchy sex thing he has all planned out for us."

"We could—" Marshall starts, but a loud meow from the back seat interrupts him.

"If you could hear us, you shouldn't have let us think you were asleep," Marshall barks to the back seat.

I sigh, "What did he say?"

Ezra transforms and leans forward to say, "I said…"

"Seatbelt!" Marshall snaps, "and underwear."

Ezra sighs, "Okay, okay, okay. I said, 'I still don't understand how it's so cold during mating season…'"

"Ezra, I told you, it's because we're in the northern hemisphere."

"You said all that in a 'meow'?" I ask.

"It wasn't just a meow, babe. Marshall, I still don't get it. You're gonna have to make one of those videos of yours about it. Anyway," Ezra leans forward and puts his hand on Marshall's shoulder, "there's no need to talk about it. I'm ready. We can try."

"Really?!" Marshall says, his ears and tail shooting upward and grazing the car's ceiling.

"Yeah," Ezra shrugs. "I know you're getting old, bro, and that biological clock is ticking. I won't make you wait anymore."

Marshall opens his mouth to protest, but Ezra interrupts, "Before you even say anything about me being older, semen doesn't give a shit about time travel. My swimmers are younger. That's a fact. But anyway, when we first met you said I'd be sitting on the sidelines stroking my cock while you filled Adley with so much of your seed you were gonna start a whole colony of hybrids. That doesn't sound so bad now." He shrugs and leans back, before launching himself forward again to muss Marshall's hair and add, "I hope they get my hair, though."

EZRA

Marshall's mouth quirks in that subtle way that passes for laughter with him. He's wanted this for a while. We all agreed we wanted to try to have kids, but none of us could agree on the timeline. Marshall was ready pretty quickly, but Adley and I have been holding out. Maybe I'm not ready, but I'm ready to make them happy and ready to grow up—or at least try. The thought doesn't scare the shit out of me anymore, and I suspect that's about as ready as anyone gets.

"I'm worried we aren't genetically compatible and our chromosomes won't pair nicely during meiosis. My field of study was Physics, not biology. I don't know enough about our DNA sequence to feel confident we can procreate with Adley. And, obviously, the internet will be no help," Marshall says, looking out the side of the window. As is usual with Marshall, now that he's gotten what he wants, he has to over-analyze it and start worrying.

Adley, knowing his tendencies, as this is a trait she shares, speaks up first, "We talked about this, Marsh. We'll speak to a geneticist first. Tons of couples can't conceive. We will have options." She always tries the logic approach. Let's see if I have to try mine: the approach of seduction and jokes.

Marshall bites his thumbnail, a new nervous tic he has established when he can't shake his leg because there's a tablet in his lap.

"Is that what's actually bothering you, Marsh?" she asks.

"I'm worried I'll be like my dad," he responds, not breaking his gaze from the horizon.

"Listen to me, Marshall. You are not like him, and you never will be. I'm serious," she says.

They both do this. They run through every possible worst-case scenario. Sometimes they get so bogged down in the worst-case scenario, they assume it's the "only logical conclusion," or whatever. That's when the doom spiraling happens, and everything starts to feel hopeless to them. They struggle to tell when something is not really a fact but just their brain trying to make sense of a feeling they don't realize they're having. And that's when I swoop in with hugs and jokes—and an appropriate therapy-inspired catch phrase for good measure.

"But what if—" he begins.

"Come on, bro! Daddy Marshmallow will be the best dad," I say, reaching forward and gripping his shoulder.

"If you don't put on your seatbelt, we're pulling over," he scolds.

"See! You're just proving my point, bro. There's no way a man so concerned with my safety could ever hurt a child."

"Ezra, please put on your seatbelt," Adley chimes in.

I buckle my seatbelt and say, "Shorts and seatbelt are now on!" I raise the shade and look out the window. The landscape outside has transformed. We aren't even that far from our home in Minneapolis, and it already feels like another world. Adley's country, Adley's world, is so much larger than mine and Marshall's. Is every corner of it so vastly different than the next?

I snap out of it to reassure Marshall, "But anyway, you don't have to worry about that, Marsh. We're a team, remember? What's that you always say about how we make up for each other's shortcomings? This will be no different. Together, you and I will make one fucking awesome dad."

There's that smile again. His jittering subsides slightly, and the idea of being a dad with Marshall eases my anxiety around the whole thing, too. They'll need someone to teach them how to pack a car, after all. And all that science shit.

"I get it, Marsh. I'm scared I'll be like my parents, too. But I think, maybe that desire tells us we won't be, ya know?" Adley adds. Adley has only recently been opening up about the parents she never talks to.

To say Adley leans sad is a bit of an understatement. She's finally found a therapist that she likes, and they've been doing a lot of work on discovering why she reacts the way she does. It seems to be helping. She has this tendency to think everyone hates her or is going to hurt her. Which makes sense. Apparently, she grew up with a mother who blamed her for literally everything and an abusive father. As an adult, her romantic and professional relationships weren't much better.

She's trying to teach herself to "assume positive intent," and it's made living with her a lot easier. Whenever Marshall or I are in a bad mood, her gut reaction is still to assume we're mad at her, but now she at least asks why we're mad, instead of assuming we're mad at her. Marshall and I have realized we do the same thing to an extent, so we're all working on it in our own ways.

"Honestly, same. I'm gonna lavish these theoretical children with so much praise I might give them some other kind of personality disorder," I say, reflecting on my own parents' shortcomings.

"We'll help each other be the best parents we can…," Marshall says, and he goes back to sketching unconsciously on this iPad with his left hand while the right drums quietly on the door, tapping to the rhythm of some object he's likely counting outside the window.

I lean forward to see what he's sketching. I don't know how he's able to do this without even looking down. It is quite amazing. He's scratching out pictures of Adley walking down the aisle and the rolling landscape in quick, economical strokes. I whisper in his ear so Adley can't hear, "You forgot those rock-hard nipples, bro," and point at the drawing of Adley.

"No, I didn't," he says with that tit-ogling smirk and swipes the screen to reveal sketches emphasizing the fabric stretching over her marvelous tits.

"Nice," I say, giving him a slow, playful punch to the shoulder. He leans into it, appreciating the praise and the touch.

"Oh, wow," Adley says, and I think she's caught us being pervs, but when Marshall follows suit with a "Wow, is that really a lake?" I look up. The vast expanse of Lake Superior begins to fill the view of the front windshield, the last remnants of the setting sun dancing over the surface.

"I am excited to explore a new city," Marshall says, marveling at the sights as the road winds closer to the shore and the trees thin to reveal more water stretching to the horizon.

"Me, too! I've never been to Duluth," Adley says.

I lean forward and place my hand on the back of Marshall's neck; he leans back so that his ear is toward me. I whisper, "We'll be doing a different kind of exploring tonight."

Marshall blushes, not quite knowing how to handle me coming at him with the full force of my pickup lines.

"Will I be the one on the sideline stroking herself for once?" Adley quips.

"Nah, babe. We gotta fill you with our seed, remember?" I respond.

"I'm still on the pill. Even if I stopped taking it tonight, I probably couldn't get pregnant yet. Plus, we really should talk to a geneticist before we try," she rambles at me.

Instead of explaining to her I was joking, I say, "Well, I suppose we'll just have to practice tonight, then."

We cross a bridge over impossibly blue water when Sexy Samuel says we have 20 minutes until we reach our destination.

"Almost there," Adley says, twisting the wheel under her hands. I lean back, but my hand remains on Marshall's shoulder, thumb tracing small circles at the base of his neck.

I pull out my phone to take a selfie video, angling the phone to capture us all in the frame. "Alright, Marsh, this is for our future children, so keep it PG." He rolls his eyes at me. "The honeymoon officially begins, babes. Wait...I can't call them babes. What should I call them? Kiddos? Tonight is gonna be epic, kiddos. Marsh, you think Adley will finally let us film her?"

"Well, now we can't show children this video," Adley sighs, annoyed with my antics.

"It's fine; Marshall will just edit it for me," I say, adjusting the angle to ensure I get the perfect shot of me and my mates.

4

MARSHALL

The GPS announces our arrival with its admittedly sexy voice. Tall pines press in on either side of us, adding to the anticipation of what this place will look like. Ezra puts the rest of his clothes on and immediately continues filming. When the lake and cabin finally reveal themselves, emerging from the trees like a vision from some architectural dream, Adley lets out an audible breath.

"Adley, Marshall," Ezra narrates to his phone in that grandiose voice he always uses for the camera, "welcome to honeymoon headquarters."

The cabin stands before us, neither imposingly large nor disappointingly modest. I'm surprised how non-ostentatious it is, given Ezra booked this. However, the ocean-like lake behind it could make even a shack look picturesque. The cabin has expansive windows that reflect the surrounding trees like dark mirrors, and a large wraparound porch that hugs the entire structure.

Adley cuts the engine, and for a moment we all sit in appreciative silence, taking in the scene.

I exit the car and walk toward the back to get our bags, but Ezra rushes me, stopping me in my tracks. "Wait, bro, come see the place first." He grabs my hand and drags me away from the trunk.

Ezra hovers next to me as he waits for Adley and me to retrieve our purse and satchel, respectively. I glance at him and consider reaching toward him, hugging him, nuzzling into his shoulder, and letting him comfort me— asking him to reassure me he won't leave. I could get him to reassure me that he does actually love me, and his plans for tonight are an act of love, not just something he's doing because he feels obligated to now that we've had the ceremony. But I don't. I simply tighten my grip on my bag's handle and look at the cabin and the surrounding scenery.

As we walk toward the cabin, Ezra leaps in front of us, sweeping his phone around to capture our faces. "First impressions from my new husband and wife?"

My eyes move across the structure. I sigh out, "Craftsman-inspired. Post and beam construction. Thoughtfully situated for optimal natural light."

21

"This guy loves wood and light, I don't know what to tell you, kiddos," Ezra stage-whispers to his phone. "I'll save the wood-loving jokes for a more appropriate audience," he chuckles.

"I hope you can contain yourself better when we actually have children, Ezra," I sigh.

"Hey, I'll have 14 months to get used to the idea of being a dad. I'm sure I can develop some restraint in that time."

"14 months?" Adley asks.

"Oh my God, please don't tell me humans are pregnant for more than 14 months," Ezra exclaims.

"No, thank God," Adley says, stretching after the long drive. "Only nine." I wonder how long the gestation period for a human-Ailura fetus would be. If genetically possible, probably somewhere in between. My mind races through all the possibilities of our genetic coupling—tripling? And my worrying ramps up. This is what I want. I want children. It's consumed my thoughts. Deciding we would take the next steps felt like the thing that would calm me. But why am I still anxious? More anxious? Why do I always do this? I want to voice my anxieties, but I can't ruin tonight for them. I can't ruin it for myself.

Adley pulls on her hat, shivering, and says, "Let's get inside. It's too cold."

Ezra continues his narration as we walk up the steps to the porch, his commentary a mixture of genuine appreciation and performative enthusiasm for whoever may eventually view this video he's making.

"The listing said a lockbox should be…" Ezra consults his phone, scrolling through the reservation details, "…under the ceramic frog to the right of the door."

I locate the small metal box and enter the combination while Ezra reads the numbers. The satisfying click of the lockbox opening and revealing the key to the cabin makes my heart race with excitement.

"That frog is a pretty obvious place to hide a key," I say.

"At least it didn't have 1234 as the combination," Ezra says, glancing at Adley with a teasing smirk.

"No one expects 1234 to actually be a password. It's perfect," Adley says, shrugging. "Plus, what are people gonna find if they break into my phone? A bunch of pictures of my cats?"

Ignoring the cat statement, I add, "Your bank account information. Those nudes you sent us last week. The nudes Ezra sent you. The nudes I sent you. The nudes—"

Adley interrupts, "Okay, okay, we send a lot of nudes. I get it, Marshall. I was joking." She says she gets it, like she agrees with me and will change her password, but I know she won't.

"Moment of truth," Ezra says, positioning himself to capture our entrance as I place the newly acquired key in the door. "Our first steps into marital bliss."

The door swings open, revealing an interior that draws distinct sounds of appreciation from each of us. It's an open concept, with the kitchen, dining area, and living room flowing together. I'm particularly entranced by the cathedral ceiling supported by massive exposed beams that look like they'd be fun to climb. I scan the surrounding area and look for a path up, but am disappointed to find there isn't one. Shame. Sitting up there and soaking up the sun might have been nice.

Honey-colored wood covers nearly every surface. I can't wait to see the rays of sunlight streaming through the windows that stretch from floor to ceiling along the far wall. I place my satchel at the door and meander forward, admiring the place.

"Holy shit," Ezra whispers, momentarily forgetting his theoretical child audience. He pans his phone slowly across the space, capturing the stone fireplace that dominates one wall. In true Ezra fashion, he jumps over the back of the plush sectional sofa. It's been arranged to maximize the view of the fireplace and the panorama beyond the windows. The breathtaking view reveals tall, glorious trees on one side and the expansive, glorious lake on the other.

The dining table looks carved from a single massive slab of wood. I approach it slowly, drawn to it, and caress the surface. I drop to the ground to eye its lines, fascinated by the joinery. It appears constructed without visible nails or screws.

"Wow, this place is going to be gorgeous in the morning!" Adley says, slowly admiring the space, her fingers trailing over the various textures of the place. She approaches the couch Ezra is on, running her fingers through his hair as she passes and stopping at the huge windows to admire the moonlit view.

"This is…" she begins, but words fail her.

"Worth every penny," Ezra says, jumping up from his position to hug her from behind and peer out the window with her, resting his head on top of her head.

I walk toward them, examining a piece of wall art—a metal sculpture that captures the undulating shape of Lake Superior with surprising emotional resonance—on my way. I slip my arm between them, bringing Adley into a deep hug, and placing my head on Ezra's shoulder. In the same way he's trying to be more affectionate with me, I'm also trying to be with him. Affection has never been something I've been good at. A few weeks ago, Adley told me, "Whenever you look at us and think, 'I love them,' that's a good time to hug us—unless we're mad."

We disperse to explore further. Ezra's filming continues as he bounds up the stairs to the loft bedroom. "Kiddos, prepare yourselves," Ezra announces from above, followed by a delighted whoop. "The bed is bigger than our current bedroom. This may be the bed you get conceived in." I presume the whoop was him jumping into it.

"Ezra, I told you, I can't get pregnant tonight!" Adley shouts up to him.

"I know, babe," he says with a wink poking his head over the loft's rails.

Adley and I move more methodically through the space than Ezra does. I'm cataloging details so I can sketch the space later. As I walk, I examine the subtle variations in the wooden floorboards and note where each one creaks. I stop to admire the arrangement of stones in the fireplace, placed with deliberate asymmetry that somehow achieves perfect balance. It all looks hand-made, subtly imperfect—beautiful. Perfect in its imperfection.

I place my hand on the cool stone and appreciate the way it feels against my hand. I close my eyes and take a deep breath. The tension in my shoulders, which I didn't even realize was there, releases. I think I finally understand what Adley means by "focus on the now." The goal is to pay attention to what's happening now, not what has happened or what might happen. Touching this stone and admiring the artistry of the cabin brings me relief and reduces the thoughts racing in my mind.

I open my eyes and turn to see Adley exploring the kitchen. Its spacious countertops and high-end appliances seem to draw her in. She opens cabinets to examine their contents. How she studies the things in her surroundings, raking them with her eyes and hands, reminds me of myself. She's so beautiful. She's so kind. Whenever she hugs me to her chest, her warmth spreads through my whole body, engulfing me in her love. I've never felt that before.

Ezra's footsteps drum quietly upstairs, in that rhythmic gait I recognize as his, drawing my attention. He's mine. They're mine. I am so fucking lucky. They love me. Me. I'm not unlovable. I'm not useless. I just needed to find them. I don't need children to feel loved. I am loved. Whether we can or can't have children, we'll still have each other—my fears about tonight ease. I can't worry about what will happen, because they won't leave me. They won't hurt me. They'll protect me the same way I protect them. I'm grateful and eager for the rest of our lives, the good and the bad, because we'll be together.

"Marshall," Adley calls, "the kitchen seems to have all the cookware we'd need." Now that elation replaces my agitation, I comfortably slide to her side, pulling her into a hug.

"I'm excited to cook here," I say, mentally adjusting my planned meals to take advantage of the high-quality tools.

I glance at my watch, "It's getting late. I should probably make dinner soon. Are you hungry?"

Ezra's footsteps thunder back down the stairs, his face flushed with excitement. He collides with the island, using its solid structure to slow his speed. "There's a jetted tub big enough for all of us," he announces, waving his phone to include his virtual audience in the discovery. "And the shower has multiple heads. Multiple. Heads."

"Is that a euphemism?" Adley asks dryly, though the corner of her mouth twitches with amusement.

"It will be later," Ezra replies with a suggestive waggle of his eyebrows. He turns to his phone. "And that, dear future children, is where the video I make for you ends. Some aspects of honeymoon life must remain private."

With a flourish, he finally puts the phone down, placing it on the counter. Without the camera, his expression shifts subtly—still excited, but with a quiet wonder indicating he's taking in the sight of the place now that he's stopped filming.

"So, do we approve?" he asks, wrapping an arm around Adley.

Ezra's hand glides over mine, which was already resting on the small of Adley's back. My fingers flinch at the touch, but I don't pull away. "It exceeds specifications," I say.

"High praise from our resident perfectionist," Ezra says, leaning into me.

"I'm the perfectionist?!" I ask, genuinely confused.

Adley chimes in, "I vote we get the luggage, unpack the essentials, open that bottle of champagne we brought, and order dinner for delivery." I was hoping to cook for them. But we would have to go to the grocery store first. I consider the time. She's right, ordering would be the best option. I don't want my desire to feed them to derail the rest of the night.

We unload enough for the night, leaving the bulk of the unpacking for later. We move together with the efficiency of people accustomed to sharing space as we bring in bags and establish our presence in this temporary home.

When the basic unpacking is complete, we reconvene in the main room. Adley orders dinner for us while Ezra fiddles with the champagne, and I find glasses in the kitchen. Ezra tries to look suave when he pops the cork, but he makes it look like he was a millimeter from causing some sort of disaster as the cork flies to the ceiling.

While we wait for dinner to arrive, Adley slides open the curtains to the deck further, letting in the view of expansive water. "This place is perfect, Ezra," she says.

"Only the best for my mates," he says, rushing to hug her, "Spouses? What are we going to call each other?"

"I think I prefer mates," Adley says, giggling at the kisses he places on her.

"Same," Ezra says. "Marsh?"

"Mates," I say, my eyes watering at the idea that they're my mates.

5

ADLEY

We sit back, pleased with the meal and feeling a slight buzz from the champagne. "I think," Ezra says, his voice low enough to seep into my core, "that it's time to test that shower. The one with the—"

"Multiple heads," I say, a smile playing at my lips as Marshall collects our dirty dishes. "You've mentioned it approximately twelve times since we arrived. I'm guessing there is some surprise up there waiting for us?"

"Am I that transparent?" Ezra asks.

"Always have been," I giggle.

Marshall returns to his seat. His hand covers mine on the table, and he absentmindedly traces small circles around the ring and mate mark he placed on my right hand. He seems to have relaxed significantly, and I don't think it's just from the champagne. Perhaps because of our chat in the car? "I took a look at the water heater. It's huge," Marshall interjects. "We can do all sorts of 'funny business' without worrying about the water getting cold. We should also be able to fill the tub." He looks at Ezra with a knowing grin.

Ezra laughs, "Only you would consider water capacity sexy talk, Marsh."

"I don't want a cold shower ruining our night," Marshall shrugs.

Ezra smiles at him, obviously picturing what our night has in store for us. "Shall we?" Ezra asks, extending a hand toward Marshall and me, with a flourishing bow.

We follow him upstairs, footsteps synchronized as we climb toward the bathroom. The space reveals itself as Ezra flicks on the softest setting of the dimmer. Ezra knows Marshall and I are not fans of harsh lighting, so he instinctively dims the light in every room we enter. The small gesture is a reminder of why I love him so fucking much.

He leads us to the bathroom attached to the bedroom. It's an expansive room tiled in slate and glass. A shower stall with multiple heads positioned at different heights dominates the room. It makes the one we have at home look positively cramped. Fuck, I think it might be bigger than our entire bathroom. Beside it is a huge jetted tub I'm surprised isn't heart-shaped. It really gives the "fuck a few people in me" vibe. Rose petals cover the whole room, and all of our various toiletries are in their appropriate place, no doubt the work of Ezra.

"How'd you have time to set this up?" I ask.

"When Marshall and I were getting the bags. I got the one for up here first and then just stopped helping," he says with a grin.

"I wondered where you disappeared to," Marshall shrugs. "But, honestly, it was quicker without your assistance," he makes air quotes at the word assistance, "so I didn't search for you."

Ezra turns to us, his hands finding the buttons of his shirt first. A private show begins as he unveils himself to us. If it were anyone else, his theatrics may border on the unsexy in how over-the-top and silly they are. But, honestly, he's so fucking hot, he can get away with murder—sexy murder—because everything he does is sexy, even this goofy little strip tease.

"I've been thinking about this all day," Ezra confesses, as his confident fingers work methodically down his torso.

Marshall watches, still as stone but for the quickening rise and fall of his chest. His dick raises to attention, tenting his pants. Since Marshall wears his emotions on his tail, it also raises to attention, matching the vibe. He purrs at the sight of Ezra, eliciting a reciprocal purr. Marshall moves behind me, his hands gripping my waist, steadying me—or perhaps himself. He presses against me, grinding against me, relieving the pressure in his pants on my back.

"Your turn," Ezra says to Marshall, shirt discarded. Deep shadows emphasize his bare chest, despite the low light. He approaches Marshall from behind. I turn to Marshall, so I can watch as Ezra's fingers find the hem of Marshall's sweater and draw it slowly upward. Marshall lifts his arms as Ezra reveals his lean, muscular torso. Each inch the sweater rises sends sparks through my body.

I step closer, my fingers tracing a path on the newly exposed skin. Goosebumps rise in their wake, and Marshall lets out an unrestrained moan. I marvel at how Marshall's body still responds to my touch as if he's never been touched before.

Ezra rests his face against Marshall's bare back and hugs him around the waist, no doubt grinding against him as he closes his eyes.

"And you," Marshall says to me, his quiet voice carrying unexpected authority. He had a bit of alcohol, so perhaps we'll see a bit of Alpha Marshall tonight. His hands move to the buttons of my cardigan with the same precision he applies to everything—methodical, intentional. Ezra leaves his spot behind Marshall and circles behind me. He gathers my hair to one side and kisses the spot right under my ear, gently rubbing the small of my back, relishing the feel of a backside without a tail. Marshall works his way down the row of buttons, slow, teasing, making sure to savor every moment, moaning as each button reveals more of me to him.

My breath catches, suspended between their complementary touches—Marshall's deliberate unveiling and Ezra's spontaneous worship. Ezra's waiting hands catch my cardigan as it slips from my shoulders. He folds it and leans to place it on the nearby countertop.

We continue this way, a ritual of disrobing that's become second nature. Some of the desperate, fumbling desire that once described our undressings is now replaced by familiarity. You'd think this routineness would remove the passion from it. That the commonplace would dull it by its lack of novelty. But something about it increases the sensuality. Our comfort with each other, our knowing each other, is now more like an intimate coordinated dance, each of us removing the edges of insecurity from the others. There's almost an erotic efficiency in it.

There's intimacy in the even practical parts of our undressing, like how we lean on one while the other helps us remove our socks. We take our time with each other, making even mundane, unsexy reveals, like removing socks and watches, seductive. Marshall kneels to remove my leggings, brushing the inside of my knee with his lips. I remove Ezra's pants and giggle at how he insists on folding them, like he did my sweater. I can never tell when he will dub a piece important enough to fold and place on a surface, rather than just let it drop to the floor, and it's almost become a game between Marshall and me to see if we can predict it. Our success rate is so low, I'd never place odds on it.

It's all so comfortable in its domestic familiarity. A dance we've performed multiple times. There's no shame—no self-consciousness. Each of us knows the other's strengths and weaknesses. Each of us knows the other's turn-ons and turn-offs. We know how to arouse and strip each other with maximum efficiency—both in the timing sense and the arousing sense. And, while it might not be sexy in its newness, its sexiness lies in the comfort of being loved. Lust is now replaced with intimacy, and, honestly, I prefer this. It's a level of arousal I've never experienced because I've never felt so known, so seen, so protected and cared for. It helps me to remove any hangups I once had. Hangups, I didn't even realize I had around sex.

When we stand bare before each other, the air between us thickens with the sound of their synchronized purrs. We embrace, appreciating the feel of our skin against each other, enveloped in arms, sound, and warm breaths.

"I love you both so much," Ezra says, in a tone more serious than usual.

"We love you, too," Marshall and I respond, speaking for each other.

Marshall reaches past us to turn on the shower, carefully adjusting the temperature. Steam rises like an invitation, further enveloping us in a level of comfort that makes me want to fall asleep a little.

"Remember our first shower together, Adley? When you were there, spit-roasting between the two of us, did you think you'd eventually marry us?" Ezra asks, breaking the quiet comfort.

I groan and respond, "Well, I didn't think you'd be reminiscing about something as unromantic as 'spit-roasting,' that's for sure."

"Babe, that was the first time I felt your lips around my cock. I shall cherish that memory for eternity," he responds, not acknowledging that the word is the unromantic part.

Ezra steps into the shower first. His gasp of pleasure as the water hits his skin draws Marshall and me forward. "Jesus, that's good," he breathes, tilting his face toward one of the ceiling-mounted heads. Water slicks his blond waves against his scalp and flattens his tail. He looks so fucking hot I can't help but launch myself onto him. Marshall has the same instinct.

Marshall and I surprise Ezra when our bodies collide with his. We press against him in the way he usually does to me, and kiss him on opposite sides of his neck. Our hands press together on his chest, gently pushing him back against the wall as we grind and kiss. I lift my leg slightly, rubbing my clit on his leg as I bury my face in the side of his chest under his arm. I love how he smells after a long day and want to enjoy it before it washes away.

The glass door closes behind us. I'm unsure who closed it until I see Marshall's tail slinking away from the handle. He, unlike Ezra, can manipulate light objects with it.

Water cascades over our bodies in rivulets that follow the contours of muscle and curve. It streams down our faces, catching in eyelashes, tracing paths across lips that seek flesh with increasing urgency. Steam wraps us in a private cloud that seems to exist outside of time. It obscures the world beyond the glass enclosure, creating a universe that contains only the three of us. It's as if, this time, we all walked through a portal together—a portal at the entrance to this shower.

For long moments, we simply exist in the sensation: hot water streaming over newly exposed skin; steam rising around us; the subtle scent of cedar from the built-in bench along one wall; the mingling of each other's musk; the vibrations of their purrs rippling through our bodies; Ezra's hands fisting our hair; my and Marshall's hands locked on Ezra's chest; and our mouths eagerly lapping at the smooth flesh of Ezra's neck.

Ezra's hand runs down our backs, squeezing our asses to pull us closer to him. He presses against the small of my back, making it easier to grind against him. Marshall moans so loudly that I can feel it vibrate in my chest when Ezra's hand runs up the length of his tail. Spurred by his touch, Marshall and my hands run downward, side-by-side, until they reach the base of Ezra's cock. With stacked fists, we slowly squeeze and pump up his shaft.

Ezra leverages the cool tile wall at his back to thrust forward in one, slow, needy push into our fists around his cock. I kiss low. Marshall kisses high. I focus on the lines formed between Ezra's clearly defined abs. Marshall works on his neck, chest, and face.

Ezra catches our wrists, stopping our strokes as they increase in speed. He brings our hands to his lips and kisses our knuckles. "You're going to make me cum," he murmurs against our skin. His thumb finds the ring and mate mark he placed on me, gently stroking it in appreciation and awe.

"That's the idea," we reply in unison. Whenever Marshall and I sync on Ezra, he gets a bit too overwhelmed and struggles to maintain the "I can't cum first" pledge to himself. Marshall and I do have an unspoken goal of trying to make him climax before us, but so far, we've been unsuccessful. It appears tonight will not be the exception.

Marshall moves behind me, his body a solid presence against my back, his arousal evident against the curve of my spine. His lips find my shoulder, then trace a path up the side of my neck as his hands circle to cup my breasts. His thumbs brush across my nipples in a gesture that is familiar and electric.

I turn in the circle of his arms, rising on tiptoes to find his mouth. Our kiss deepened immediately, the restraint of the day giving way to a hunger that demands satisfaction. Ezra presses against Marshall's back, his lips finding the sensitive skin behind Marshall's vestigial ear, his arms roaming over us both.

We shift configurations with fluid ease—Ezra turning to take my mouth while Marshall's teeth graze Ezra's shoulder. Marshall and Ezra share a kiss of such intensity that I can almost feel it myself. Our coordination wanes as we each eagerly try to press against the others, eager to place our mouths on flesh. Eventually, I'm caught between them, my back against Marshall's chest while Ezra kneels before me, his mouth exploring the sensitive skin of my stomach. I lurch forward, grinding thin air as he teases at the spot just above my sex in that way he learned long ago will drive me crazy with need.

Ezra breaks from our tangle of limbs and lips and reaches for the soap, a bar of something expensive and herb-scented. He works it between his palms until a lather forms. Marshall outstretches his hands, silently requesting the soap so that he and Ezra can wash me. However, instead of handing the soap to Marshall, as he usually would, he hands it to me.

The surprise on Marshall's face is evident, his hand still outstretched, when Ezra reaches toward Marshall and lathers his chest instead. I rub the soap between my palms, smile at Marshall, and rub the suds across his back.

Ezra's told me of his plans to be more intimate with Marshall tonight. Marshall's general sexual passivity makes him not ask for what he wants, so things tend to focus on me or Ezra. Ezra and I agreed we should let our encounters focus more on Marshall occasionally, especially tonight. We don't want Marshall to feel like he's always at the bottom of the hierarchy. Of course, during this conversation, Ezra joked about how he would let Marshall be a different kind of bottom. We've pledged to find ways to help Marshall feel like he has as much power and worth in this relationship as we do.

Ezra's hands move across Marshall's shoulders as the two lock eyes. When they're purring together, they seem to have this uncanny ability to speak to each other without words. The way Marshall's face melts under Ezra's gaze and the way he maintains eye contact make me think this may be one of those moments. Ezra's hands roam down Marshall's chest, around to his back, swiping over mine—confident touches that speak of understanding and deep appreciation. Marshall closes his eyes, surrendering to the sensation of his two mates cleaning him, and his body relaxes incrementally beneath our ministrations.

I stand on my tiptoes and breathe, "Tonight, we worship you, Marshall. What do you want?"

"I like this," Marshall moans out.

"This really all you want, bro?" Ezra whispers seductively.

6

EZRA

Marshall opens his eyes and looks at me, his eyes only flitting to mine momentarily before settling on my nose. The discomfort he usually has around eye contact does not wane in this moment.

"I want...," he says as he looks down at the space between us. He's not great at asking for what he wants. I know it. And the fact that he can't look me in the eye right now tells me he won't have the bravery to ask for it tonight.

I hover in front of him, standing just far enough away that our dicks don't touch each other. I run my hand up to his hair and grip it a little forcefully.

"It's okay, Marshmallow, I know what you want," I say. He wants me just to tell him what to do. He wants me to want him, and he wants me just to take him. My attraction to him is still not at the level I think he'd prefer, but I do love him and want to make him happy. I want to please him. It's a different kind of attraction. It's not a sexual draw, but an emotional one. But his desire for me and devotion to me make me want to give him whatever he wants. And it is supremely hot to see this man, who's a little bigger than me, whimper at my touch as I pull his hair. It makes me feel powerful, and stiffens my dick in a way I never thought possible until I met him.

I usually just take, but not tonight. Tonight, I'm going to give him exactly what he wants. Me.

I silently nod to Adley, signaling to proceed with the plan. She'll comfort him—relax him—make him melt into those soft tits and sweet cunt, while I take him. Operation Melt that Marshmallow is a go. She grabs his tail, placing it between her breasts. He moans at her touch as she brings her body close to his, pressing her breasts against his back. She rubs her hands along his side, teasing at the area right next to his cock, massaging his thighs.

With my free hand, I palm his face and look at him. His eyes cast downward. How he balks and submits to me makes me want to devour him. His eyes, partially closed like this, emphasize the length of his dark eyelashes against his cheeks. The way gravity pulls the corners of his mouth downward, slightly stretching the skin across his cheeks, when I tilt his head like this, makes him look so delicate. So adorable. He really is handsome once you see past the hair he hides behind and the general dork vibe he exudes. Overcome by how cute he is, I gently kiss his jaw, eliciting another whimper and causing him to meet my eyes. I slowly close the space between us and watch his face, knowing how much he likes to watch his body join Adley's, assuming he'll want the same with mine.

I step closer, shifting my positioning, ensuring that our dicks slowly graze against each other as I bring my body to his. When our chests come together, he gasps and meets my eyes again before returning his gaze to the area between our bodies. Only for a moment, before I fully press our bodies together, the space between us reveals just the tips of our dicks, side-by-side, our abdomens hiding the rest. His eyes widen at the sight. The desperate way his breath quickens, squeezes our cocks together between us, massaging them gently while they stay gripped between our pelvises. Adley's arms reach around, encircling us both only momentarily before they return to him.

I release his hair, causing his posture to loosen, as I run my hand down his neck and shoulders to continue washing him. I begin with his back, my touches tentative and teasing at first, then increasingly bold as I feel him respond. The subtle arch of his back, thrusting him toward me, as I find a sensitive spot along his spine, spurs me. When my fingers work circles at the nape of his neck, a low hum of appreciation increases the volume of his purr. The vibration resonates in my belly and makes my cock twitch between us, appreciating the feel of him.

I press gentle kisses against him, not yet being aggressive with him, relishing in the moans and thrusts that show he wants more. In this moment, I'm so aroused, I think I wouldn't mind him pulling that Alpha Marshall out of himself for my fluffy ass, but that's for another night.

He stands frozen, a sentinel, letting Adley and me wash him. Once Adley steps away, his tail, with a mind of its own and now free from the cage of her breasts, wraps around my leg. My wet tail lies limp behind me, heavy from the water weighing down my fur, making it hard to move. His hands finally rise, his desire outweighing his uncertainty. He grips my hips, still not looking at me, but taking a little of what he wants. I kiss his neck in response, hoping this will let him know I am okay with him touching me. He doesn't need to ask permission. He has permission. But, I know that's likely not enough, so I say, "You can touch me, Marsh. Take what you want." His hand trembles at my side and moves to my wet tail before it gently pets the base of it—causing me to thrust closer to him. I knew he loved my tail.

Adley has a lathered washcloth and rubs it all over our combined bodies, washing us. I wrap my arms around his lower back and kiss him—really kiss him. He moans into my mouth and wraps me in his powerful arms, making me buck against him, ready to sink myself into him.

He startles, breaking from our kiss to look back at Adley. By the way his dick jumps on my stomach, I assume she has begun washing his ass.

I pull myself away, missing the feel of him against my cock and chest, missing the taste of him. With a final peck on the jaw, I say, "I'm going to wash Adley for you, Marsh," not wanting to leave him.

I push him against the shower wall, not too forcefully, but more forcefully than I would with Adley. He likes things a bit rougher than she does. His hands linger on my waist as I step away, unwilling to let me go.

I accept the soap from Adley. The rings Marshall placed on our right hands catch against each other slightly, and our fingers linger together momentarily in the exchange—my mates.

I grab another washcloth and position Adley so Marshall can watch what I do to her. I rub the cloth over her body and kiss her neck, glancing up to see his reaction. I pay particular attention to the areas around her breasts and inner thighs. She moans and writhes under my touch. Her breasts heaving as she leans back into me, slowly stroking my cock. I spread her lips for him to see as I lather her with soap.

Marshall simply watches, enjoying the pleasure of my presenting her to him. He doesn't even stroke himself; he just waits. The rigidity of his posture has diminished, and he leans languidly against the wall—consuming us with his eyes.

Adley turns, placing her hands on the wall opposite Marshall, and raises her ass in the air while flipping her hair around so that her whole back is exposed to us. I run the washcloth through her backside, enjoying the show as the water runs through her crack. My fingers tease at the tight opening behind the cloth. I must enter one of my mates soon, or I may explode.

Marshall seems unable to stifle his hunger any longer and pushes himself off the wall toward us, finally ready to take what he wants.

MARSHALL

The sight of Ezra washing Adley, and the pleasure on her face as he kept his eyes locked on me, stirred a deep desire in me to leap, bite, and fuck. Some primal desire that is likely as much instinct as it is lust.

I press my dick against Adley's ass, wrapping my arms around her to grope her breasts. I lick the nape of her neck and let my teeth graze against her skin. I pull back slightly, readying my cock to sink into her tight cunt, but Ezra spins her out of my arms, to have her stand with her back against the wall. He grabs my cock, squeezing and rolling his thumb over the tip. He gently pushes me toward her with his other hand and says, "I got her ready for you, Marshall."

He releases my cock, and I launch toward her to press my body against her, kissing her hard on the mouth. I grind against her, ready to take what is mine. Take what is ours.

"Wrap your legs around his waist. Let him take you against the wall, Adley," Ezra says. I note the distinct way he's phrased this. Usually, he'd tell me to fuck her against the wall. Usually, he tells me what to do. I don't know if I've ever heard him tell her what to do.

Adley wraps her hands around my neck and lifts herself. I grip her ass and assist her up the wall, gliding my cock through her folds as I hoist her. Once she's high enough that my tip knocks at her entrance, she wraps her legs around me. I cradle her ass and watch our bodies intertwine as she sinks deep onto my cock. The way my dick pierces through her body, parting her lips as she takes my length, is literally the most beautiful thing I've ever seen, despite it also being the most obscene thing I've ever seen.

I press my chest against her, feeling those full breasts against me as I take a moment to appreciate the pleasure of her walls wrapped around my cock. I stand there, with her pinned against the tile, and don't move, I just savor. She grabs my hair and, with both hands, pulls me into a hard kiss. Our tongues intertwine, and we moan in unison. I buck unconsciously into her. The moans that resonate through her breasts feel like a purr of her own, spurring my desire to pump slowly into her, seeking a release within her. As her tongue swirls against my teeth, I think about how she's both the first and last person ever to slip their tongue in my mouth. And now she's mine. Not all mine, but mine, nonetheless.

Ezra turns off the shower head that sprays against my back. I'm not sure why. I turn to look to see what he's doing. Usually, I know exactly what he's doing as our purrs synchronize our desire and motivation to please Adley. But, for some reason, I can't predict his next movement.

Adley grabs my ears and turns me toward her, breaking my gaze from him. "Your cock feels so good inside me, Marshall," she sighs into my mouth.

I thrust within her, pushing her up and down the wall, relishing in the feel of her clenching against my cock. I bend so her tits can bounce against my face, as I move her up and down the wall. She claws at my back, and I take a breast in my mouth, eliciting a "Oh, Marshall, yes," from her. I open my eyes to see Ezra at my side, his hand pumping lube along his length as he watches me fuck her. He rests his hand gently at the small of my back above my tail, startling me out of my breast-bouncing trance. Oh, shit. Is he going to do it now? Am I ready?

Ezra has hinted, and by hinted I mean outright stated via crude jokes, that he will be entering me tonight. I've wanted it for so long, too afraid to ask directly, except when I've had a bit of alcohol and become what we all dub "Alpha Marshall" (a.k.a. "Brave Marshall" a.k.a. "Actually says what he wants Marshall").

He breathes into my ear, "Now I'm going to take you. Do you want that, Marshall?" Yes, I'm ready.

"Yes," I groan, with Adley's breast still in my mouth. When I feel Ezra's hand against my inner thigh, I stop thrusting within her. I tremble a little, and Adley hugs my head against her breasts, comforting me in this moment of exhilarating fear. I've thought of this moment every day since I was too young to even understand what I was imagining Ezra doing to me. Thoughts of him atop me, pushing my tail to the side and biting the back of my neck, accompanied every orgasm I had before I met Adley.

I freeze, and my focus is entirely on the feel of his hand sliding between my buttocks, lubing my entrance. I whimper into Adley's neck and might cry tears of joy. I worry I may drop Adley when my knees go weak. "You set the pace, okay, Marshall," he says as he gently presses a finger into me.

"Oh, God," I say, pressing deeper into Adley. The combined sensation is so incredibly overwhelming that my vision blacks out momentarily.

"Tell me if it's too much. I'm serious, Marshall. You have to communicate," he says, rolling his finger inside me and bringing his body against mine. I nuzzle into Adley's throat and cry out as pleasure waves throughout my entire body.

"Okay," I rasp out, not sure I actually will—willing to let him do whatever he wants to my body.

Ezra kisses Adley over my shoulder, and I join their kiss. Now accustomed to his touch within me, I want more. I buck inside Adley, grinding her against the wall, seeking the pleasure my body desires.

"More?" Ezra asks, sensing from my body language that I want more, but knowing I won't actually ask for what I want him to do.

God, yes, please, I need you inside me. I need your chest pressed against my back. I nod, my face buried in Adley's neck.

"Say it, Marshall," he says, "I need you to tell me what you want. Do you want my cock?"

"Yes," I moan into Adley's tits. She strokes both sets of my ears, slowly, as I pant into her chest. Her heart pounds against my cheek, and I close my eyes, waiting for what's next.

"Good boy," he says into my ear, causing my heart to stop. He glides behind me, lightly kissing my back as he positions himself. He unwraps Adley's legs around my waist, causing her to spread further as he moves closer behind me. I grab her legs instinctively, hooking under them and pinning her to the wall. I grind deeper into her. She exhales in that way that tells me I'm pushing the air out of her. Ezra pushes my tail to the side, and gently presses his lubed dick against my entrance. I'm so incredibly aroused at the idea of Ezra fucking me, I almost climax before he's even done it.

The tip of his dick pushes forward and a deep pressure begins to fill me as he slowly enters me. The moment his head passes my entrance, and his girth begins to slide into me, sends sparks through my whole body. His moan resonates through his chest against my back, and his breath warms my nape. Every part of my body stiffens as I allow the pleasure of the sensations to overwhelm me.

Adley kisses my neck as I remain frozen, letting him fill me. He pushes me slightly forward, shifting my weight and causing me to fill her even deeper.

"Does it feel good, Marshall?" she asks, petting my head gently while she wraps me in a loving embrace that, if it weren't completely demented, I'd say was almost motherly.

"Oh, God, yes," I respond into her neck. When Ezra's full length is within me and his balls press against me, my tail, which had tensed at my side, relaxes and wraps around his waist.

"You're taking me so well, Marshall," Ezra says at the back of my neck, placing a kiss on my hairline. "Is this what you wanted?" he growls slightly, pulling my hair to tilt my head and forcing my eyes to meet his. I will myself to maintain the gaze.

I choke out, "Oh, God, yes. For so long."

"That's my good boy," he says, kissing the spot under my vestigial ear. "My little Marshmallow."

Ezra hooks his arms under my armpits, gripping my shoulders and shifting his weight so that he can sink even deeper into me, which I didn't realize was possible. He rests his full weight on me, and now I'm the one thing keeping us all from falling—I don't know if I can, I'm so overwhelmed with happiness and pleasure I want to sink to the ground, cry, and release all over the walls of this shower.

They both wait, letting me adjust, kissing me and kissing each other. He drops his chin to my shoulder. His breath is ragged as he waits for me. Adley's breath matches his, and I can tell they are using all their willpower not to take over.

He grazes the back of my neck with his teeth. My body responds by instinctively pushing back on his cock. When I've pushed so far that the feeling is almost too much, I retract and push forward into Adley's heat. When the feeling within her peaks, I pull back, only to thrust further onto Ezra's cock. I almost can't take the pleasure. When I pull away from one overwhelming sensation, I'm pushed into another equally overwhelming one. My body is a pendulum, swinging between high points—a metronome of pleasure. I'm so delirious that I can't remember the difference between kinetic and potential energy to make the appropriate metaphor. Which we all know, I would have struggled with even if I wasn't locked between my two mates.

My thrusts shift from tentative to desperate as I learn the rhythm and how far I can go in both directions before it's too much. Eventually, it's not too much in either direction. It's not enough, and I pump back and forth, taking what I want.

I bury my face in Adley's tits, and thrust into her so deeply she starts to wail at each push. She reaches down between us, and rubs at her clit. "That's right, fuck me, Marshall. Take it," she says, closing her eyes and tilting her head back on the wall.

I can tell by the way her hand moves and her body convulses that she's close to coming. Her pussy clenches around my cock, squeezing me in that perfect way. Ezra is on my back, a dead weight, as I push against him. He claws at my side and grips my hips, keeping our two bodies locked so I don't buck him off me. With each thrust backward, he moans and whimpers against my neck.

I unravel my tail around his waist and trace the tip inside his leg. When I tickle his opening, he wails, "Oh, fuck," and rocks within me at the same rhythm as I rock into Adley—unable to remain dead weight any longer. As her walls contract around me and his dick twitches within me, I thrust harder, grunting and snorting into her breasts as I fully lose myself to the primality of it all.

I'm desperate to climax and bite my lip so hard it might bleed. Adley wails out in pleasure as her orgasm clenches around my cock making my thick ropes of pleasure finally release within her.

I feel a sharp, delicious pain on the back of my neck as Ezra bites down and fills me with his own warm seed. My orgasm, which I thought had already reached its full heights, spreads through the rest of my body, not just centralized around my dick. Ezra moans around the spot where his teeth connect with my neck. I groan so loudly that I startle Adley, before she smiles and wraps her hands around my neck, pulling me into a deep kiss and prolonging my pleasure.

My orgasm lasts longer than theirs, still washing over my body as they are coming down from their own, and for a moment, I worry I may be stuck in a permanent state of euphoria. Just as I think I might black out, the climax subsides, and I fall limp against Adley.

Ezra steps back first, removing himself from me and turning the showerhead back on, letting the water hit my back again. My eyes close as sleep threatens to overtake me. Ezra helps me remove myself from Adley, and it takes every ounce of strength I have left to shift my weight to the wall. Ezra catches her as she slips her legs to the ground and helps her steady herself. After Adley is safely on the ground, Ezra grabs my shoulders and walks me so I can sit at the bench. I lie back against the wall, boneless, unable to hold myself up anymore. I close my eyes and doze as they fuss over me—cleaning me, petting me, praising me, and loving me.

7

ADLEY

Marshall sits listlessly on the bench, head lolled against the wall, watching Ezra and me continue bathing. I've never seen Marshall need so much time recovering, and the goofy grin on his face rivals the one he wore the morning after our first time together. "I think we broke Marshall," I laugh to Ezra as I rinse the last of the conditioner out of my hair.

I lean forward and push Marshall's hair out of his face, checking to ensure we rinsed him thoroughly. His eyes lock on my hanging tits and his dick rises to attention the moment Ezra presses his dick against my pussy and strokes my clit.

"All clean, babe. You didn't think we'd let you just come once, did you?" Ezra says behind me.

Marshall grabs my hand and kisses my ring finger, stroking his cock with his free hand. "What kind of husbands would we be if we did that?" he asks, his energy fully returning.

"I don't always have to come multiple times, guys. It's been a long day. Let's go to sleep," I say pressing my ass back on Ezra so that his cock slides against my pussy. I'm not sure why I'm protesting, when Ezra was washing his cock a moment ago the only things that stopped me from dropping to my knees in front of him was the soap on his cock and the fear of shampoo getting in my eye.

"Nonsense, babe. Marshall and I already agreed that you'll be coming more times tonight than you ever have," Ezra moans into my back.

"How many concurrent schemes do you have running right now, Ezra?" I ask with a giggle, my eyes raking over Marshall.

"Lost count. Just like I hope you lose count tonight," Ezra says, knocking his dick at my entrance, waiting to see if this protesting of mine is an act or if I don't want to come again.

"Well, you did mention spit roasting earlier," I say, eyeing Marshall's cock, "that sounds kinda appetizing."

Marshall's eyes widen as he gets my meaning. I bend down and lick the tip of his dick, eliciting a moan. Ezra needs no further invitation and plunges his dick inside me the moment my lips part to take Marshall's length down my throat.

I rake my nails down Marshall's thighs, causing a gentle thrust from his hips. I close my eyes and sink as far as I can, letting him touch the back of my throat. I pull back and suck as hard as I can.

"You like this view, Marsh. You like seeing your husband fuck your wife on your cock?" Ezra asks.

"Yeah," Marshall responds.

"Describe it to me. Paint me a picture," Ezra says, thrusting into me. Ezra recently discovered a new quirk of Marshall's: the reduction of anxiety that he experiences after an orgasm seems to unlock a part of his brain that allows him to be incredibly poetic.

"An angel leans before me, her seraphic hair cascading across my thighs as she takes my dick in her mouth. Her pillowy soft lips rise and fall around my shaft, and when she brings them as far down as she can, I can see the stars from whence she obviously came. Her otherworldly breasts hang below her, swaying with a rhythm set by the devil behind her. He smirks at me, ethereal in his own right, proud of defiling such a heavenly creature."

"Damn, bro, we gotta start writing this stuff down," Ezra whispers into my back as he kisses against my spine. The relentless, thorough way in which Ezra works my clit reaches a crescendo of pleasure. I moan around Marshall's cock, as my orgasm clenches around Ezra's.

"That's my girl," Ezra says, quickening his pace into me, intensifying my orgasm as he fills me with the warmth of his semen. "Come with us, Marshall," he says, and as if on command, Marshall releases to the back of my throat.

=^..^= ♥ =^..^=

Ezra turns off the water, and the sudden absence of its rhythmic thumping leaves an emptiness in my head. Marshall reaches for the plush towels hanging nearby, wrapping one around me first, his movements gentle. Steam follows us from the shower, curling around our damp bodies.

I kneel beside the deep tub, turning on the water and testing the temperature. Marshall, unable to help himself, wipes up the water we've dripped in our short trek from the shower to the tub. Ezra slinks toward his noisily chirping phone, but he notes Marshall's nervous energy and puts it back down without a glance. He puts his hand on Marshall's shoulder, offering him a sincere smile.

"We'll all clean up together after, okay? Let's sit with her," Ezra says, relaxing Marshall.

I wasn't sure if this place would have a tub, but I was really hoping it would. I brought a few different bath oils and bubble baths, just in case. I pour oil into the water, which blooms across the surface in iridescent patterns, catching the subdued bathroom light and transforming it into something almost magical.

"Kinda looks like the portal did," Marshall says, watching the oil spread with me.

"I wish I could have seen mine," Ezra says, gently stroking my back as we watch the tub fill.

With towels wrapped around their waists, Ezra and Marshall sit on the edge of the tub, next to me, absentmindedly stroking my back as we watch the tub fill. I pour a bubble bath into the water. The bubbles rise quickly from the force of the cascading water. Despite its colossal size, the tub fills quickly.

The jets hum to life when Marshall presses a button on the control panel, sending streams of pulsing water churning through the scented bath. The bubbles grow exponentially. The sound echoes off the tiled walls, creating a cocoon of white noise that adds to the vibrations of their combined purrs.

"We should probably stop the water now," Marshall says.

"It's not full, yet," Ezra says.

"The water will displace when—" Marshall says.

"Alright, I trust you. Please, no science right now," Ezra says, turning the tub off.

As we stand to remove our towels and step in, I say, "So, I bought you boys a wedding present. It's just something small."

"Oh, yeah, babe?" Ezra asks.

"It's in the bag," I say, gesturing to the bag with bath oils. He rummages through the bag and finds a small vial with a ribbon tied on it; he squints at it momentarily, reading the text. He refuses to admit he needs glasses. "Adley, babe, what are you trying to do to us?" Ezra laughs.

"I dunno. I thought maybe a drop in the water would kinda be like CBD oil is for humans," I shrug.

Ezra holds the offending bottle of Catnip essential oils to show Marshall. "What do you think, Marsh? Wanna try it?"

Marshall briefly considers it, gripping his towel at his side, and says, "Yeah, let's try it. But just a drop."

"I'll let you do it, babe. I don't trust myself with it," Ezra says, handing me the bottle.

They step away as I unscrew the lid, distancing themselves from the fumes. Before placing a drop in the tub, I wait and watch their reaction. The bottle has a near-instant effect on them, despite the distance they put between themselves and it. Their faces transform with languid expressions and dilated pupils. They trade soft touches—fingers passing over damp skin, caressing with lingering attention. The way they caress each other is so gentle and affectionate, it's heartbreakingly sweet.

Ezra stands on tiptoes to rub his face against the top of Marshall's head, scenting him and nibbling at his ears. Marshall balances him with steady hands at his waist. They let their towels drop to the ground and bring their bodies together, rubbing their faces along each other's bodies. It's so fucking hot. I want to sit here and watch them, but I place a drop in the tub and close the lid, feeling like letting them go much further, just for my enjoyment, may skirt the definitions of consent. Slowly snapping out of it, they walk toward me and inhale the scent of the bath.

"That's nice," Ezra says, stroking his dick absentmindedly. "Relaxing. Not too much, though."

"Yeah," Marshall says, placing his head on Ezra's shoulder and stroking his dick distractedly, as well.

"You sure it's not too much? You both still seem a bit…," I say, pointing a finger between their two stroking cocks.

"Nah, babe, I'm good. I've got my wits now. Ladies first," Ezra says, extending his hand to help me into the tub. I slip beneath the surface with a sigh of pleasure, the hot water immediately beginning to work my muscles tired from travel and stress.

"Marsh," Ezra says, elbowing Marsh with the hand stroking his cock, "check out how her tits float."

Marshall simply grunts and approaches the tub. He steps in carefully, settling next to me, his longer limbs folding gracefully into the space. He places his head on my shoulder, moaning as the jets hit his back. As if lost in a dreamy sleep, he closes his eyes and strokes my nipple floating at the water's surface.

"Don't fall asleep yet, bro," Ezra says, following him into the tub. He positions himself on the other side of me and places his head on my other shoulder. He closes his eyes and strokes my other breast.

They purr and moan peacefully at my side. I lean back, ready to embrace the warm blanket of the water and perhaps fall asleep. I tip my head back against the tub's edge and close my eyes in absolute bliss.

"Maybe we should look into getting a new place…one with a bathtub," Marshall says, moaning as he sinks deeper into the tub.

For several minutes, we simply soak in contented silence, allowing the jets to massage away the last traces of anxiety and loosen our muscles. Marshall's free hand, not at my breast, finds mine beneath the water. He strokes the ring around my finger, and his purr deepens. Ezra's fingers trail languidly over my skin beneath the silky water.

Marshall shifts, turning towards me. His lips find my neck, planting tender kisses along my sensitive flesh. "I love you, Adley," he murmurs against my skin.

"And I love you, Adley," Ezra purrs, his breath tickling against my ear.

"I love you two, too," I sigh out.

We doze in tranquility, when Ezra jolts up, "We can't fall asleep. If we're in here too long, it'll dehydrate our skin."

"Is that really true?" Marshall asks.

"Hey, I didn't argue with you about the sciencey tub filling thing. Don't argue with me about skin."

"Alright," Marshall says.

"A few more minutes, then. I'm looking forward to passing out in that gigantic bed," I say, re-closing my eyes.

Marshall hums in agreement, his hand gliding down my side beneath the water to rest on my hip. He shifts, bringing his lips to the sensitive spot just below my jaw. I sigh as he sucks gently, sending shivers through my body.

Ezra captures my lips in a deep kiss, his tongue teasing my lower lip. I part my lips, welcoming him in as desire pools low in my abdomen. His hands cup my breasts, thumbing circles around my nipples until they harden beneath his touch.

Marshall's fingers lower, skimming along my thigh before dipping between my legs. He strokes my folds, teasing me with featherlight caresses.

I moan softly as Ezra's hand slides down my body, his fingers seeking the junction between my thighs and joining Marshall's inside me.

Reaching out, I take each of their hard cocks in my hands, stroking them slowly beneath the water. They groan in unison, hips rocking into my touch.

Marshall leans in, capturing one of my nipples between his lips as his fingers mingle with Ezra's in my folds. I gasp, back arching as they circle my clit with knowing strokes.

Ezra moves to straddle my hips, his hard length brushing against my stomach. He takes Marshall's face in his free hand, bringing their mouths together in a searing kiss. I watch, transfixed, as their tongues dance and teeth nip at their lips. I thrust against their fingers, turned so the fuck on by their kissing above me.

Pulling back, Ezra shifts forward, the head of his cock nudging at my entrance. Slowly, he sinks into my pussy, stretching and filling me as Marshall maintains a solid pressure on my clit. I moan, my hands gripping Ezra's hips as he moves in deep, rolling thrusts.

Marshall's fingers match Ezra's rhythm, stroking and circling my clit with increasing pressure. The dual sensations send me spiraling higher, my body caught between them.

Marshall dips his head, tongue swirling around my other nipple before drawing it into his mouth to suck. I thread my fingers through his hair, holding him close as he lavishes attention on my breasts.

Ezra's thrusts grow more urgent, his breathing ragged against my neck. "Fuck, you feel incredible," he pants, angling his hips to hit that perfect spot inside me. I cry out, my walls fluttering around him as the pressure builds.

Marshall shifts, rising slightly out of the water, to capture Ezra's lips in another fierce kiss. I watch as their tongues tangle, hands roaming over water-slicked skin. Ezra reaches down, wrapping his fingers around Marshall's straining erection. The three of us kiss, tongues intertwining as I scream out at the pleasure they bring me.

"I want you both," I moan, the words barely a whisper. "Please…"

Marshall rises out of the water, sitting on the tub's edge beside me and grabbing the bottle of lube. He covers his member, preparing himself to enter me. He swings his legs behind me so that I nestle between his thighs.

Ezra grips behind my knees, lifting me, while Marshall lifts me from my armpits. They slowly lower me onto Marshall's cock. Marshall moans as he enters my backside, the vibrations sending aftershocks coursing through me. Ezra returns to his position in my pussy.

After recovering from his entrance, Marshall returns to his mission on my clit—increasing pressure. Ezra's pace grows erratic, his fingers digging into my hips as he nears his peak. I am thrown over the edge, and we all embrace in a shared kiss as I scream into my orgasm.

With a guttural groan, Ezra spills himself inside me, his cock pulsing with each wave of pleasure. At the sounds of our pleasure, Marshall drives into me deeper, his own release pulsing hot inside me.

8

MARSHALL

Ezra rises first, water streaming from his body as he reaches for fresh towels hanging nearby. I help Adley stand, my hands tremble slightly, muscles so relaxed from the multiple orgasms, and the dreamy, catnip bath. Ezra wraps a towel around Adley with his usual tenderness toward her. He then gives me one and allows me to wrap myself. We help Adley climb out of the tub and step out ourselves, our longer limbs and strength making the process easier for us.

"Damn it," Ezra says as he climbs out of the draining tub.

"What's wrong?" I ask.

"We both came in her," he says.

"And that's a bad thing, because?"

"We wanted to see if mate marking her made her pussy taste like us now. It's obviously going to now that our spunk is all up in her," Ezra says.

"Gross, Ez," Adley says.

Damn. I did want to know if she tasted like him now. Oh, well. I'm sure I'll find out soon enough.

Ezra hands us yet more towels to help us dry our hair and tails. Adley wraps her hair in a towel. Ezra and I, in a practiced coordinated effort of soft touches and towel pats (never rubs, or else Ezra will freak), help each other dry our tails. In this moment, I'm struck by the simple domesticity of this intimate dance he and I have perfected. Our touches convey something different than they once did. Instead of lust, need, or even hate, it's a desire to assist, protect, comfort, and love. Adley once told me I show her I love her in lots of little ways. I didn't see how he and I do that for each other until now.

I grip Ezra's tail through the towel, relishing in the feel of my hand wrapped around its girth. His skin is still damp, and his hair is curling. He turns and winks at me. I am so overcome with love for him. The sight of him illuminated by dim lighting overwhelms me. I drop the towel to the ground and wrap my arms around his waist, hugging him, placing my chin on his shoulder. He uses the towel he's holding to tousle my hair gently. I rasp out behind choked tears, "I still can't believe you're mine."

"Believe it, Marshmallow," he says, the nickname symbolizing sincerity. He still struggles to show me outright affection, and not calling me "bro" is usually the first sign he's trying.

He brushes the hair that falls into my face out of my eyes and smiles at me. "Was that okay, Marsh? You feel alright?"

"Yes, thank you, Ezra. It was perfect," I say, closing my eyes and hugging him tighter. He squirms, no doubt eager to put his multitude of lotions on and hair products in, but he doesn't pull away. He lets me hug him and continues to dry me gently.

"Everything you dreamed of while you stroked yourself in that lab?" he asks with a chuckle.

"Flawless," I whisper into his back, knowing he somehow thinks flawless is better than perfect and not a synonym.

Adley approaches from behind and wraps her arms around us, placing her face on my slightly damp back. "Group hug," Adley says as she squeezes us toward her.

"You're both so beautiful," I say, my voice catching. "How did I get so lucky?"

"We're lucky, too, Marsh," Adley says, kissing my back.

Tears roll from my eyes, coating Ezra's back. He straightens his stance and turns, wiping the tear from my face with his thumb like he usually does for Adley. Only for a moment, he looks at me like he looks at her. He aggressively hugs me, breaking the moment and wrapping his arms around my shoulders. It's a hug that still has lingering discomfort with affection, masked by less tenderness, but he's trying. I'm so grateful for his love.

ADLEY

"That bath was too relaxing. I'm going to fall asleep the moment my head hits Adley's pillowy tits. Now that we're mate-bonded, I suppose I can let you two see how I look if I fall asleep with wet hair," Ezra says. He throws his towel to the side and leaps onto the bed the way he always does, splaying out and making snow angels in the sheets.

He transforms, picking at the bed with his claws, ready to get comfortable when his phone makes a noise on the nightstand. Ezra, unable to resist the pull of his chiming phone any longer, rises and walks over to the nightstand. He hovers over it and paws at the screen.

"Seriously, Ezra? Can't you just mute it?" Marshall says. Ezra meows at him in that tone that usually translates to worry.

Before Marshall can translate, Ezra transforms and brings his phone close to his face. God, he really needs glasses. Stephanie has called me 30 times. What is going on?" His face contorts in fear, multiple worst-case scenarios obviously flashing through his brain. "It might be important," he says to us—the question in the statement is apparent. He's supposed to avoid work as much as possible, and his tone clearly asks if he can call her.

"You should probably call her back," I say, worried. Ezra looks at Marshall for further permission.

"It's fine," Marshall says, doing that shoulder shrug, which means he's acquiescing but not happy about it. "It's probably important."

"It'll just be a sec, I promise," Ezra says, his phone already calling her. He squeezes Marshall's shoulder as he passes him. "Hey, Stephanie, what's going on? Why are you demon dialing me?" he asks as he walks to the adjoining bathroom.

"I hope everything is okay," Marshall says as we get into bed. He settles onto his usual side, and I place my head in the crook of his shoulder, pulling him into a hug. He kisses me on my head and rubs my shoulders.

"You going to be able to sleep tonight, Marsh?" I ask, knowing he struggles with insomnia.

"I think so. That catnip in the bath was a good idea. Might have solved my insomnia," he says with a chuckle, his eyes already closed. The multiple orgasms probably won't hurt, either.

Ezra's previously hushed voice rises in urgency and breaks through the bathroom barrier: "What are you talking about?!"

Marshall's eyes fly open, and we share a concerned look. We freeze, eavesdropping on the call.

"What!? Holy shit. Yeah, yeah, okay," Ezra says, now sounding panicked.

We rise from our languid poses as Ezra returns to the room, shorts now on. Shit, he got dressed? Something bad is happening.

"Yeah, I'll watch it right now. I gotta talk to Marshall and Adley about this. Yeah. Yeah. Thanks, Steph. Bye," he says, hanging up. He stands, speechless, looking at us, his hands limp at his side, mouth agape. Speechless is not a state we usually see him in.

"There's…there's a congresswoman. She's…," Ezra says, unable to articulate what he's thinking. "Steph sent a video. We have to watch it." He climbs into the bed, squeezing between us, and opening his messages. Ignoring the hundreds of texts, he finds the one from Stephanie with a video and opens it. He holds his phone over his face for us all to see.

A gorgeous woman stands at a podium, fiddling with papers and talking to the group behind her, whom I presume is her family. "Oh, that's Crystal Beck. She's a congresswoman from Minnesota. She's super progressive. I love her," I say, while we wait for her to speak.

"Who's that? He looks familiar," Marshall says, pointing to one of the two extremely attractive men flanking her sides. One has pitch black hair rimmed with white around his temples and sideburns. The other wears a fedora that appears to hide brown hair. They both have a weirdly familiar air about them. The black-haired man embraces Congresswoman Beck and speaks to her in a hushed tone, eliciting a loving, contented grin that visibly relaxes her.

I recognize him and say, "That's her husband. She's all over social media. He shows up in a lot of her videos. You've probably seen him on the news or social media or something."

"I don't think that's it…," Marshall responds, his voice trailing off. His eyebrows knit as they do when he's trying to remember something.

The other man joins in on the small talk. He doesn't embrace her, but stands stoic at her side. He must give her a pep talk because she nods and appears invigorated. Interesting.

She kisses the three children and takes her place at the podium, while the two men return to their initial positions.

She finally speaks, "Thank you all for being here today. I stand before you as a citizen who deeply loves our country. Like so many of you, I dream of an America where everyone can live a full, meaningful life—no matter who they are, or where they come from. After many conversations with my family, friends, and supporters, I made an important decision. Today, I am proud to announce that I am officially running for President of the United States of America."

"Why would Stephanie send you this? What does this have to do with you?" I ask, confused, while the congresswoman describes the platform she plans to run on.

"Just wait," Ezra says anxiously.

She spends a few moments bullet-pointing her platform before continuing, "I have one more announcement." She pauses, her speech

51

faltering for the first time. She clears her throat to continue, "Concerning my husband, Sebastian. As I've said, I'm running on a platform rooted in the belief that everyone in the United States deserves the chance to live their best lives. That includes people who, despite living and working here, are denied a pathway to legal citizenship. These are hardworking, law-abiding individuals who contribute to our communities. Yet they are held back by unjust laws. Unjust laws that make it nearly impossible for them to fully live, work, and love within this country." She pauses again, this time not as a falter, but for dramatic effect. She deepens her voice and pounds her hand on the podium, "I believe it's time for a change. I want to make citizenship more accessible for all people, regardless of the country...or universe...they come from."

Universe? We look at each other and hold our breaths, awaiting her next words.

"My husband and thousands of others living across this country are from another universe. They appeared in this world without any documentation proving their existence or place of birth. Due to their lack of documentation, they are unable to become citizens—"

Someone from the crowd interrupts her speech, unable to accept what she is saying and breaking the standard protocol of a press conference, "Are you joking?"

She goes off-script to respond, "No. I am not joking." She straightens her back and continues, her voice firm. "Approximately 20 years ago, my husband and his best friend," she says, motioning to the man on her other side, "came through a portal to our world. We have determined that there are thousands of others in this world, in this country specifically, with similar stories. People who contribute, who belong, but are invisible under the current laws. For them, citizenship isn't just difficult, it's impossible. That's why I'm making this issue a pillar of my platform. I plan to expand the path to citizenship for these individuals, for all individuals who seek to build a life here. If you crossed a border or a portal to get here, you deserve the same rights, the same recognition, and the same chance to thrive as anyone else. I'm now open for questions." She stands, waiting for what she said to sink in and bracing for the onslaught of questions. Her poise doesn't falter, but she does grip the edges of the podium.

"This is ridiculous. How can you expect us to believe this?" a reporter, now turned heckler, calls out, not waiting to be called upon.

She seems to have expected this reaction. She nods to her husband, who moves to stand beside her. She places her hand on his shoulder, and they lock eyes. His stern face melts, and they smile at each other, emanating pure love and adoration.

"These people are not just from another universe. They also have the ability to transform into...cats." Her husband and the other man cringe at the word "cat," their trained charisma and camera-readiness flinching momentarily.

The crowd laughs uproariously.

Her husband grips his black hair and pulls it off his head. It fully lifts off, revealing a wig cap. He was wearing a wig? He removes the wig cap, exposing snow-white hair and snow-white ears nestled within it.

"Damn, that wig is a good idea. Wish we had thought of it," Ezra says absentmindedly.

"I know who he is!" Marshall exclaims. "That's President Angora! The President, who supposedly committed suicide with his best friend and campaign manager after losing his second-term election."

"Fuck, I don't remember. I sucked at history...," Ezra responds, pausing the video.

"He died before finishing his term, leaving his Vice President, President Chartreux, to finish his term. Chartreux expanded on his policies, leading to the most progressive reforms in our country's history," Marshall says excitedly.

"Umm, I remember Chartreux, everyone knows him, but I don't remember Angora...," Ezra says, trailing off.

Marshall taps the video to make it continue playing. The congresswoman nods to the handsome man at her other side. He removes his fedora, revealing brown ears in his matching brown hair.

"That's not a cat. That is just a man wearing cat ears. How is this supposed to convince us? Ezra From Another World's ears are more convincing than those," someone laughs.

"This is their humanoid form. However, they can transform into a cat-like form. They will demonstrate. However, they cannot transform back to this form on camera."

Another impatient reporter calls out, "Because its bullshit."

"Because they would be naked if they were to transform back," she says flatly.

She nods to her husband and squeezes his hand. He instantly transforms into a long-haired, snow-white cat.

The crowd gasps.

"Oh, my God! I know who he is now. Didn't he die…well, disappear, like, over a hundred years ago?" Ezra asks. Of course, he'd remember the long-haired president.

"Yes," Marshall says, dumbfounded.

The other handsome man accompanying the congresswoman also transforms, causing more questions as the two strut on stage. Eventually, they both go off-screen momentarily before returning in their anthro forms, with their tails and ears no longer hidden, and their bodies reclothed. We watch the rest of the video in stunned silence, engrossed in the spectacle.

Eventually, the questions turned to the legitimacy of the children who, at first glance, appear perfectly human. She's been the picture of powerful stoicism throughout the speech, but when asked about her children, her mask drops and she speaks less forcefully. "Yes, my children are part-Ailura…They are American citizens by all rights bestowed upon those born in this country. They are afforded all the protections that entail," she says protectively, obviously afraid this whole spectacle will turn her entire family into science experiments.

The scene devolves into controlled chaos. With questions hurled at the congresswoman and her husband, she deflects gracefully, answering the questions as they come. Eventually, she says she will take no more questions and circles her children in her arms. She ushers them off the stage, flanked by her husband and his best friend.

The video ends when the cameraman who filmed the whole thing, and seems too hot to be behind the camera, enters the frame. An even more handsome male news anchor comes to his side and hugs him close. They remove their hats to reveal that they, too, are Ailura before cutting the feed.

Ezra turns off his phone, and his arms collapse at his side. Ezra tells us, "Apparently, this happened a few hours ago. My accounts are being bombarded with people asking if I'm really 'from another world' and if Marshall and I can transform into cats. Videos of other Ailura coming out are flooding socials—there are so many of them. Stephanie said the congresswoman emailed me a few weeks ago. Steph ignored the email, assuming it was just a donation request. I guess my coming out stirred this whole thing up. They were hoping I could assist them today…I wish I had seen that email."

"Well, fuck," Marshall says.

"Yeah, fuck," Ezra and I say in unison.

"Things are gonna be a lot different now," Ezra reflects.

We all sit with this information for a long time, contemplating what it means for our lives and our futures—worrying about the repercussions.

Never one to be able to sit in silence for long, Ezra snuggles into me, dick hard against my leg, and says, "Well, Adley, might as well stop that pill. Looks like we can put some hybrids in you."

Marshall leaps to hover over us both and adds, "Let's get started."

=^..^=   ♥   =^..^=

Want to learn how Crystal Beck ended up with two fated mates and followed her dreams to become a congresswoman?

Stay tuned for the next installment of Cozy Clowder Chronicles!

Subscribe to my newsletter for more info:

https://www.imogenknowed.com/newsletter

A Note from the Author

Hello, readers! Thank you so much for reading Whispers, Whiskers, & Wedding Night. I published Whispers, Whiskers, & Wine almost six months ago, and these three still consume my thoughts! I missed them terribly, and I just had to revisit them to see how their relationship evolved.

I used this book to expand upon some things that had to be cut from the original story for length and pace, and I am so happy that you are now able to see a fuller story of these characters' lives and psyches.

Thank you so much for your support. Please review this book and Whispers, Whiskers, & Wine on Amazon and Goodreads. Reviews help indie authors like me creep our way into the algorithms we can't afford to buy into and make it easier for us to write more books!

If you'd like to keep up with my work, follow me on social media and subscribe to my newsletter:

https://www.instagram.com/imogenknowed/
https://www.imogenknowed.com/newsletter

About the Author

 Imogen Knowed has suffered from insomnia since she was a little girl. So, she has a lot of free time on her hands—especially at night. She spends her days programming video games and her nights reading and writing smut. She particularly enjoys reading webtoons and is a dedicated follower of quite a few long-running series. When she's not writing smut or making video games, she's hanging out with her daughter, husband, dog, and/or three cats.

You can follow her on social media:
https://www.tiktok.com/@imogenknowed
https://www.instagram.com/imogenknowed/

Made in the USA
Monee, IL
29 June 2025

20199499R00039